BROKEN

JAE JOHNSON

ISBN: 0692317902
ISBN-13: 978-0692317907

DEDICATION

To my cheerleaders and my champions
Dustin, Jill, Jim, Madison, Karen, Renee, Charles,
Carolyn, Teresa and Tiffany
Because I couldn't be Jae without your help, encouragement, support and love!

CHAPTER 1

Erica sat across from her therapist in an oversized leather chair and picked absentmindedly at the heel of her designer boot. She was only seeing Dr. Delia Boyd because Daddy threatened to cut off her trust fund if she didn't see someone – other than her playthings – for her obsession. And, of course, Daddy insisted that she had to be a *female* therapist. Erica had already seduced each man who tried to "help" her with her issues. Seducing the weak-minded do-gooders was much easier than delving into her perceived issues -- and it was a lot more enjoyable.

Today's session was particularly annoying. She had mistakenly recounted the story of John Foster's visit to her Playhouse and her annoyance with how the evening ended. Erica had definitely wanted John, more than she'd ever wanted anyone. From the time she'd seen him in the club dancing with that unworthy wife of his, Amelia, Erica knew that John was different than the other men she'd encountered. He knew how to pay proper attention to a woman; she could see that in the way his hands roamed his wife's body. John knew how to respect a woman; she witnessed that when he pulled her to the privacy of their booth before going any further on the dance floor. But most of all, John Foster knew how to be true to a woman. Nothing showed that more than his self-imposed limit during their threesome: *He would not have sex with anyone but his wife.*

Erica remembered being flabbergasted with that rule, though she didn't betray that to John and Amelia. Sure, she had wanted both of them when she brazenly approached them in their booth, but her main reason for inviting them back to her apartment that evening, if Erica was being honest with herself, was to have John inside of her, looking at her and touching her in the same way he had Amelia. She'd tried everything, completely turning up the kink factor, in hopes that he would waver in his commitment. She'd used his wife's body and put on a show that most men only got in the privacy of their homes in the dark with lotion and a porno in their DVD players. She'd also done everything to wear little miss wifey out so that when John was pulsing and ready, there would be no way her tight little marital cunt would accept him, so Erica would have had to step in and do the job. All of her efforts were to no avail. John never broke his limit. That had made Erica want him even more.

Dr. Boyd latched onto Erica's frustration like a hungry dog to a bone and refused to let go. Her question broke Erica out of her mental replay of one of the most frustrating events of her life.

"So, this man, John," Dr. Boyd began, choosing her words carefully, "You wanted him not just because you wanted to 'play' with him. You wanted to be looked at and touched like he was touching his wife."

Erica stopped picking at her boot and glared at the smug doctor sitting across from her. *What would SHE know about pleasing a man, or wanting a man, for that matter?* Dr. Boyd was plain. She sat there in her baggy, green blouse and brown

Bohemian-inspired skirt looking more like Shaggy from Scooby-Doo than the highly respected therapist she was. Her auburn hair was pulled back in a tight bun, and rimless glasses rested on her sharp nose.

Erica defiantly refused to answer.

"You wanted to be valued, to be treasured. That's what drew you so much to John."

Again, Erica sat in silence and began to squirm under her therapist's scrutiny.

That can't be right.

Erica thought back to the evening that John and Amelia ventured to her party at what she affectionately calls her Playhouse.

Erica rarely masturbated, yet she'd had to in order to clear her mind the afternoon that John's voice caressed her through her phone, telling her that he and Amelia would be coming to the gathering. His dark-green eyes had haunted her from the moment they'd met, and she couldn't get enough of the sounds he'd made deep in his throat when he was turned on or of the groans he'd made when he came. Since the brutality

4

of her first sexual experience, she rarely had one-on-one sex with anyone; after all, there was safety in numbers. Yet, she'd found herself dreaming of rolling around with John, just the two of them. The first dream caught her off guard, but she looked forward to sleep because she knew that he'd be there to worship her with his hands, his eyes and his body.

That evening, everything had been perfect. Everyone had been enjoying themselves, both in the common area of the Playhouse and in the private rooms. Her bedroom upstairs was primed with her favorite toys and lubes in preparation for John and Amelia. She'd had to dodge Brock all evening; although he was one of her favorite playthings, she was reserving all of her attention for John.

When he'd walked through the door, everything stopped around her as she took John in. White, button-up shirt opened at the collar and soaked from the rain, tailored black slacks and hair hanging in wet curls on his forehead. She wanted to take him right then and there, but the negativity coming from Amelia hit her in waves. Amelia was dressed down in a blue T-shirt – a T-shirt for heaven's sake! – and jeans. She was pretty, but, still – a T-shirt?!?!?

Erica had delighted in showing John the house, and watching him become aroused as he took in the erotic sights made her wet. His gaze lingered on the blonde twins – Di and Sky – as they took turns riding their mounts. Erica made a note that she would invite the girls to join them as soon as she got John and Amelia broken in. They would be her gift to John for forgetting his limit and for giving in to her.

Erica could sense Amelia's growing unease, so she had reluctantly left them alone. She could do patience. Sure, it wasn't a virtue she had been blessed with, but, for John, she could wait. Then, she'd seen her opening. John had left Amelia alone to get them something to drink. She'd broken up her flirtation with Brock and headed straight to John in the kitchen.

She'd stalked right up behind him before dropping her voice a seductive octave and coaxed, "Finding everything you need?"

John spun around to face her. Something unpleasant flashed across his face, but it was quickly replaced by excitement in his eyes. "Yes, thank you," he'd replied.

"Amelia seems," Erica had thought for the right word, "different." She certainly didn't want to put him on the defensive.

"She's just a little uncomfortable; I'm guessing. I'm hoping to loosen her up so that she can enjoy the evening. This is the same thing she drank at the club last week. Here's hoping," he'd said hopefully, and his enthusiasm had been contagious.

"Here's hoping," Erica had agreed and ran her finger up his stomach to his chest. "Last week was a lot of fun." Touching him brought back a flood of sensations.

"Fun? I think 'fun' is an understatement." John's laughter seduced her, and she'd laughed with him.

"Oh, John, Amelia's a lucky lady. You're such an attentive lover." Erica had never worked so hard to seduce a man, and, although she'd known it was cliché, she'd punctuated 'lover' with a nibble to her bottom lip. He rewarded her gamble with a groan that travelled the course of her body. She took her shot and wedged herself between arms that held his beer in one hand and Amelia's vodka in the other and did what Amelia's limit had denied her: She'd kissed him.

For a moment, John had given in. Her tongue took his captive as he opened his mouth to hers. He'd wanted her!

Erica remembered the emptiness she'd felt as Amelia jerked her away from John. Anger replaced the emptiness as she watched Amelia berate John and make a scene in her Playhouse. Amelia needed to go. John needed to stay. Yet, Erica knew with growing disappointment that John would leave with his wife. And he did.

That disappointment marred the face she saw peering back at her from the reflection in Dr. Boyd's glasses.

"Erica, think about that between appointments this week," Dr. Boyd instructed.

"About what?" Erica spat like the spoiled brat she was.

Dr. Boyd answered her patiently, "About what John represented to you and why you were so disappointed when you didn't get it. You wanted to be the object of his affection and devotion. You wanted to be valued and," Dr. Boyd paused for the proper effect, "loved."

Bitch.

"You have got to be kidding me. He was hot. I was denied. I wanted to fuck him. That's all," Erica argued.

"Really? Did you want John Foster, the man? Did you want the orgasm? Or, and this is what I want you to really think about, did you want to feel the love and adoration that he gave to his wife, even while fulfilling the fantasy *you* presented him?"

Erica sat there dumbfounded. Dr. Boyd couldn't be right. She simply couldn't.

Dr. Boyd glanced at her watch and then flashed Erica a satisfied smile.

"I think that about ends our time for today. I'll see you next week. Same time."

Fuck!

CHAPTER 2

Robert sat at the bar, absentmindedly peeling the label from his bottle of beer. George Thorogood sang about drinking alone, and Robert couldn't help but think that it was a very appropriate song for the mood he was in tonight. He stared at his reflection from the mirror behind the bar. He simply couldn't understand what had gone wrong with Amelia. He was a good-looking man. That wasn't conceit; he simply was. He'd always gotten any woman he'd set his mind on, and several he hadn't. He was tall, broad and chiseled. His blue eyes and wavy mess of black hair made women swoon when he combined their power with his smile. He knew it, and he used it. Still, Amelia had resisted. Her resistance left an ache in his chest with which he was unfamiliar.

Amelia was different from all of the other women in his life. Sure, she was beautiful, but that wasn't it. She had something about her that set her apart from the pack. She had warmth smoldering inside of her that reflected through her big brown eyes and touched everything she did. Her laughter heated him from the inside, and all he'd known was that he wanted to keep her near him. There was one problem. She was married. Her husband, John, frustrated Robert like nothing else. John made Amelia one of his last priorities, and the pain that caused her was evident. Never was it more evident than at the celebratory dinner the marketing firm had thrown Amelia to celebrate her promotion to account executive that John had neglected to attend. Robert had flirted before, but that night, he'd made his intentions clear to his co-worker. He would never let a woman like her feel neglected – in *any* way.

It worked for a while. Amelia had begun joining him for lunch in out-of-the-way, romantic places where he could reach out and touch her hand or brush a lock of hair from her face. Amelia's blush would deepen each time he touched her, and he knew he had an effect on her. Each time John wouldn't get home in time for dinner was a win for Robert. He didn't want Amelia to get hurt, and he knew that John was hurting her. But, it would make it all the sweeter when she would finally see that jerk of a husband for what he was and choose Robert. Before he'd realized it, he'd fallen in love with Amelia. That had been a huge mistake, and here he was now licking his wounds and fending off advances from women in the bar who would happily lick them for him.

Amelia was venom running hot in his veins. Making love to her had been his total and complete downfall. Before that, she was an infection from which he would have eventually recovered. After, well, he was finished; he didn't want the anti-venom. Like an addict with his favorite drug, all he wanted was more of her.

Amelia came to him that fateful evening completely broken by John, and she fell into his arms. When their lips met, Robert felt her heat, and he was happily consumed. This was what it was supposed to be like, and dammit, he wouldn't let go. She'd resisted for a moment, and he could feel John's hold on her. Yet, Robert didn't give up, and with one plea, she was his. They'd made love twice that night, rolling around in his bed, her scent staining his sheets. He'd been in heaven, and he'd had his very own angel in his arms to prove it. She'd seemed distant when everything was over, but Robert thought it was just nerves. She was married, after all, and had never done anything like that. As Robert watched her leave his apartment that night, he couldn't have been happier.

When he didn't get a response from his text the next morning, he had been slightly worried, but he knew that she must be struggling with the events from the evening before. Robert wanted to be there with her and help her, but he knew that Amelia needed her space. When Sunday rolled around and there was still no response, he got a little angry. Surely, Amelia hadn't used him. She wasn't like that. She was so full of love and warmth and sincerity. She was kind. *She wouldn't do that*. He'd consoled himself that evening in the sheets that still smelled like his angel and planned a sweet beginning to their workday.

He'd left early for work that Monday to stop by the local doughnut shop and get Amelia's favorite: a chocolate-covered cream-filled doughnut and a cup of steaming mocha. He took a moment and scribbled *Thank you for indulging me. XO, R* on the cup, left it on her desk inside her cubicle and waited.

What happened next had taken him completely by surprise. Amelia rejected him. Following her perfect ass to the break room so that they could talk without rousing their arriving co-workers' curiosity was like marching to the gallows. Each mention of how sorry she was tightened the noose around his neck, and he'd found it hard to breathe. By the time she got to, "I'm sorry. For everything," he'd had enough and had to get out of the noose before she kicked the precarious pedestal out from under his feet and left him dangling for his final breath.

Until that point, Robert had never intentionally said anything to hurt others. He knew how much words could hurt and linger much longer than a slap or a punch. Then again, he'd never felt for someone like he'd felt for Amelia, and so the words just poured from him.

You know what? Don't worry about it. I mean, I liked you a lot, but it's not like I'm in love with you or anything. I knew you were married. I took a shot, and I had a great time. But, you obviously want to stay with Mister-My-Job-Comes-First, so who am I to try to change your mind? Besides, the new receptionist has been making eyes at me. Maybe I'll give her a shot. See you around, Amelia. Thanks for the ride. It was fun.

Robert couldn't believe that those words had come from him as he stormed down the corridor leading to reception. He'd led Amelia to believe that he was going to hit on the new receptionist, but all he'd wanted to do was to put some space between them. He'd planned to apologize the next day, but Amelia had transferred to the office across town. That was a hard punch to his gut. He'd felt used, angry and hurt, but above all, he'd felt sad. Amelia had been the first woman he'd fallen for, and she had been the first woman to reject him. His heart didn't know how to take it, so he'd taken the rest of the day off and sat on the very barstool he now occupied and drank to erase her from his memory.

That was weeks ago, and here he was – still sitting on that same damned stool, still drinking, still remembering and still hurting. Might as well be a country song. He'd heard about Amelia's accident and wanted to rush to her side but fought that urge. It wasn't his place. She didn't need him and John fighting as she was trying to heal. He'd stayed away, and that had only deepened the ache in his chest.

Robert caught sight of his reflection again. This time, the handsome man staring back at him looked like a stranger. He didn't recognize the pain glaring back at him. Dammit. He'd get over Amelia Foster. He had to. There was no other choice. He would not wallow. He would get back out there.

Robert's thoughts went back to the receptionist at the office. Joy? Joyce? He'd always greeted her with *Good morning, Beautiful,* to avoid having to learn her name. She was pretty. She had a fantastic body, and, most of all, she was available. She'd let him know that almost daily since she'd replaced Harriet when the grey-haired grandmother had retired. She was exactly what he needed, a warm, willing woman to take his mind off Amelia. He could bury himself in her and swallow her cries of pleasure with his kisses over and over again. She would let him; of that, he had no doubt. He glanced around the bar at the other women hovering; they would *all* let him.

Why the hell wouldn't Amelia?

He would have to put that thought out of his head. There would be no Amelia. There would be others, and, somewhere in the ocean of women that lay before him would be his life preserver. She was out there. She had to be. He'd thought he'd found her, but Amelia was just a respite in the waves.

The handsome man in the mirror narrowed his eyes in determination and took the last swallow of his beer. He paid his tab and caught a cab back to his apartment. Luckily, he'd known he'd be too wasted to drive after another night at the bar thinking about *her* and took a cab instead of driving his car. The thought of leaving his 1967 Camaro in the bar's parking lot overnight was almost as unsettling to him as not having Amelia, but it was better than wrapping it and him around a tree in the drunken state he was in; they both deserved better.

Robert let the silence of his home envelop him as he closed the door behind him. This was a lover he was familiar with. *Silence.* She lured him to the couch, where he crashed. He still could not sleep in his bed. Amelia was always there, looking gorgeous in just-fucked hair and lips plump from his kisses. Each time he closed his eyes he saw her there. No, the couch had been just fine since she rejected him, and it would comfort him again tonight.

Tonight, he would sleep in a drunken stupor with the same images from his night with Amelia haunting his sleep. Thick brown hair and eyes like melted chocolate would flash like lightening in his dreams.

Yet, tomorrow…tomorrow was full of promise.

He would battle back.

Tomorrow.

"Tomorrow," he mumbled as sleep took him over.

CHAPTER 3

Erica kissed her latest playmates at the door and bid them goodbye. It was already late into the morning, and she needed coffee and a shower – in that order. She swayed into the kitchen, set up the coffee pot and leaned against the counter to wait. Soon, the intoxicating smell of the nectar wrapped around her, and she salivated while making her first cup. She sat at the table sipping her coffee as she flipped, half-heartedly, through a fashion magazine. Her thoughts drifted to her latest therapy session as she flipped through the polished pages.

Dr. Boyd couldn't be right. Hell, Erica wouldn't *let* her be right. There was no way in hell that she would give that pompous, pious, psychobabble-spouting shrink the satisfaction of being right. She'd wanted John simply because he was so fucking sexy and not for any other reason.

Still, to be looked at the way John looked at his wife must be a wonderful feeling. There was security in a look like that. There was love and dedication and trust. Sure, those words were as true as a fairytale to Erica, but, back when she'd let herself believe in fairytales as a child, those words permeated her fantasies. That look lead to happily-ever-afters.

Shit.

Erica brought herself back from traveling down that road. Fairytales weren't real, and no one got their happily-ever-after -- even with a man like John Foster -- and Erica was sure that someday, his wife would find that out.

But still…wouldn't it be nice?

Erica sighed as she rinsed her coffee cup and put it in the sink. A hot shower was just what she needed to chase away thoughts of fairytales and happy endings. Life was what you made it, and she had nothing to long for. Daddy kept her bank account nice and fluffy, just like she liked it. An accountant paid all of her bills, so she had nothing to worry about, and a cleaning crew rotated between the Playhouse and her apartment and kept them both immaculate. With a body to die for, money to burn and no worries, Erica truly lived the life of a princess. In fact, that's what Daddy affectionately called her; she was Princess, with a capital P!

Erica stepped into the shower and let the hot water run down her body. Last night had been fun, but she needed the water to help massage away any potential for soreness from her tired muscles. She'd picked up a great couple at the club downtown and brought them back to her apartment for a night of debauchery. The two were simply friends who had gone out for some fun, so there were no limits, no possessiveness. Those were Erica's favorites. Still, after the goodbye kiss for both this morning, she didn't plan to see them again. They weren't invited to her Playhouse. In fact, no one new had been invited since John and Amelia. Surely, there were worthy recruits out there. Erica just had to find them.

Challenge accepted, Erica thought to herself and giggled.

She finished her shower and was picking apart a blueberry muffin when her phone chirped. Erica picked it up. It was a text from Brock. THINKING OF YOU. As soon as she read the text, another chirp announced something new. It was a picture of Brock winking and holding his bulging penis in his hand. Erica laughed and replied,

"How romantic! I'm swooning." She clicked SEND and went back to her muffin.

Brock had been a great find. She'd met him and his short-lived girlfriend at the club and invited both back to her apartment. The night went as planned, and he was hotter and better in bed that she'd imagined. Yet, that wasn't enough to keep him and his girlfriend together after the threesome. She had broken up with Brock a few days later. Brock had taken Erica up on the invitation to the Playhouse, and the rest was history. Even though new people joined the group, Brock remained one of Erica's favorites and was consistently invited up to her private bedroom. He was one of the only people Erica trusted to have sex one-on-one with, making him very special to her.

Brock was a detective with the local police department, and he was a damned good one, too. He was recently divorced and had a little girl. His short-lived girlfriend was just one more woman in a step to get over his wife. He'd told Erica once that his wife was unable to get over the danger of his job. After his partner was killed in the line of duty, Brock had lost himself in making sure the shooter would never see the light of day instead of losing himself in his wife and assuring her that she was all he ever needed. When she asked for the divorce, she'd told him that she'd already lost him to his job, and a divorce was better than losing him to a bullet, and, just like that, they were sharing custody of their daughter and meeting on neutral turf to shuffle her from house to house every other weekend. Erica remembered thinking that it was his wife's loss. Brock was a hell of a man with a passionate, voracious sexual appetite and was smart and funny on top of it all. He was definitely her favorite playmate and the closest thing she had to a friend.

Still, with everything going for him, there was no romantic spark. He was more of a court jester who made her laugh and forget about anything that might let loneliness get to her than a prince charming. He was a big, handsome, wall of muscle with a great smile, a huge cock and the talent to use it. Erica told herself that if all she ever had in this life were her looks, her money, Brock and her court of sexual playthings, she would die a very happy woman.

Her phone chirped and brought her out of her self-satisfied musings. DINNER TONIGHT? Brock again. He certainly did try. Erica knew that he wanted more from her, but she wasn't able to give it to him. She couldn't devote herself to one man. There was no man who made her want to commit solely to him. She doubted there ever would be. Something felt broken in her, but she had no desire to find out what or how to fix it. She kept Brock happy, but she kept him at arm's length. She wasn't a touchy-feely romantic, but she didn't want to be cruel, either. NOT TONIGHT. GOING RECRUITING, she replied. His reply was almost instant. K. HAVE FUN.

Erica looked at his reply. HAVE FUN. Was she having fun lately, or was she searching? Dammit, no! Dr. Boyd's theory would not lead to some deep, dark revelation. She *was* having fun, and tonight, she would prove it to herself. Tonight, she would find someone to invite back to her Playhouse and expand her group. She needed something – someone – new to play with, and she was going to find him – or her – tonight.

Take that, Dr. Boyd! Erica thought to herself petulantly and stopped short of sticking her tongue out.

CHAPTER 4

Robert checked his teeth for remnants of his breakfast and then his breath for freshness before stepping out of his car. Today began his journey back. It was a beautiful, autumn Friday, and he was going to make *Jill's? Joy's? Joyce's?* day. Whatever her name, he was going to ask her out. She was going to say yes. She might not be THE ONE, but she would be the one important step in the right direction that he so desperately needed to take.

Robert strolled into the doors of Sebastian Treat & Associates, the premiere marketing firm in the tri-state area, and checked his reflection in the glass around him. He looked great in his dark blue V-neck sweater and fitted jeans – thank you, casual Friday. Miss Receptionist didn't stand a chance today.

"Good morning, Handsome," she purred to him as he made his way to the reception desk and leaned into her.

"Good morning, Beautiful," Robert echoed back. *What IS her name?* He looked all around for something that would tell him. He couldn't call her 'Beautiful' all night. He was a better man than that. Surely, he could get one of his co-workers to call her by name or something. Just then, he thanked the heavens for divine providence and a flirty woman. She flipped her long, blonde curls off her shoulder so that he could get a better view of her very ample cleavage and revealed his salvation – a nametag! So, it wasn't Jill, Joy or Joyce. It was Ginger. Ginger was a blonde. *A true blonde?* His mind wondered as his eyes wandered.

Ginger mistook his appreciation for his discovery as an invitation to lean in to give him a better view, but he couldn't complain there, either. How had he not noticed *those*? Ample wasn't even the half of it. With their perfect shape and surely-DD cup, he'd bet that they weren't natural, but they'd sure be a hell of a lot of fun. He must have been living in a haze to not notice them – her – before, but he was damned sure noticing them now.

Ginger giggled and brought him out of his musings. He tore his eyes from her breasts and made a point to look her in the eye. Women loved that. Ginger was no different.

"So, *Ginger*," he emphasized her name like it was the most precious thing on his lips, "I was thinking that you and I could grab some dinner tonight."

Ginger's big blue eyes opened wide with surprise. "Really?" Then, they narrowed in a challenge.

Robert held his breath. Surely, he hadn't misread two women in a row. His confidence was starting to waver.

Ginger laughed. "Well, it's about time you took a hint!"

Robert gave her his best smile, guaranteed to make women fall to their knees. *Not all women.* He was quick to quiet that part of his brain still focused on Amelia's loss and move on to the task at hand – getting Miss Ginger here out of her clothes.

After getting Ginger's address and making plans to pick her up at 7:00, Robert walked to his desk, feeling much more like himself. He'd taken his first steps to getting over Amelia, and he was on steadier legs than he thought he'd be. Of course, the thought of Ginger bouncing on top of him helped. There was no doubt in his mind that the evening would end with just that. Monday morning might be a little awkward because, although he was sure that Ginger would help him move past his heartache and be absolutely stunning doing it, he was also absolutely positive that she was a fleeting fancy, an elixir to heal his pain. Though he didn't relish using someone, he needed this. If he could be honest with her from the onset and not lead Ginger on, then this could be a lot of fun for the both of them.

And, with that thought, Robert picked up the folder for the latest campaign on his desk and laughed so loudly that everyone in the surrounding cubicles poked their heads up to make sure that he was okay.

The laughter was strange in his ears but sounded like music. It rumbled around in his chest and belly and loosened the grip that heartache had on him. It felt great.

His next thought made him laugh even harder.

I'll be damned! Mom was right! Laughter IS the best medicine!

His eyes watered with the uncontrollable laughter now booming through the office. He looked around at his co-workers, and it was apparently contagious. Everyone was starting to laugh with him

– or at him. Hell, at this very moment, as great as Robert felt, he didn't care. He just laughed until he couldn't anymore.

As Robert's laughter died down, he looked again at the folder in his hand. His newest client was Andrews Farms, home of the finest, freshest melons around! Robert doubted, after the glimpse of Ginger that he had gotten this morning, that Andrews Farms' melons were the finest, but this was surely going to be the most fun he'd had at work in a very long time.

CHAPTER 5

Erica scanned the crowd in the club for any hope of a new playmate. Though there were some gorgeous people, there just wasn't anyone she cared to see naked more than once. She took the last sip of her mineral water and stood to stretch. Tonight was obviously a scratch, but it wasn't time wasted. She'd managed to dodge a dinner date with Brock. Though she adored his friendship, she just wasn't in the mood for one-on-one tonight.

Soon after Brock's first visit to her Playhouse, Erica had tried to bring Brock hunting with her. At first, he'd seemed open to the idea, but later that evening, he'd gotten weird and possessive. That was her first clue that he wanted more than she was willing to give to him, or anyone, for that matter. After that, she'd been careful to keep Brock at a safe distance.

"Well, dammit," Erica muttered to herself after scanning the dance floor one last time. She had so been hoping to spend the evening in a sweaty knot of writhing bodies, but it looked like trashy reality TV, a bottle of wine and actual pajamas for her tonight. Until –

"Well, HELLO!" Erica thought to herself as she watched this tall, gorgeous hunk walk in with a beautiful, bottle-blonde silicone-enhanced doll on his arm. With their entrance, Erica motioned for the scantily-clad waitress to bring her another bottle of mineral water, and she sat back down and watched. Erica was always very careful when she was hunting; it was always mineral water on her lips and never alcohol.

Robert didn't really want to go dancing, but Ginger had pouted and begged over dinner. She loved dancing, and she hadn't been in such a long time. He acquiesced, thinking that having her body pressed against his on a dance floor would be great promise for the night to come. Besides, the thought of her pouting and begging brought to his mind images of her begging for his swollen cock to be caressed by her pouting lips. With that thought, Robert couldn't wait to take her dancing!

The music from the dance floor pounded in his ears and instantly put him on the defensive. He pulled Ginger closer to him, and she rewarded his chivalry with a sweet giggle. Robert weaved their way to the bar and ordered two beers and turned around, smiling broadly at his date to seal the deal.

Ginger giggled again. "You've practiced that smile a time or two; haven't you?"

"What smile?" Robert turned it up a notch and took a slow, deliberate swallow of his beer. "I don't know what on earth you're talking about." He winked one of his blue eyes, and Ginger squirmed on her stool. This evening was definitely going to end up just as he'd planned.

"Let's dance," Ginger pleaded with wide, hopeful eyes.

Robert let her hope for just a moment before giving in and leading her to the dance floor. Jason Derulo's "Talk Dirty to Me" beat around them as Ginger expertly balanced on her precariously high heels and moved up and down Robert's leg. She left nothing to the imagination as her blue eyes let Robert know that she couldn't wait to ride him the same way.

Robert growled and pulled Ginger closer to him, lifting her body effortlessly off the floor, and pulled her body up his. Her shapely legs wrapped around his waist as she ground her hips into his hardening cock. The song's rhythm sent the couple into a hedonistic frenzy as their lips met. Robert loved the way Ginger's tongue danced with his while her fingers tangled in his hair and pulled. He just knew that she was going to be a bed-full of fun! All he had to do was dance with her a bit and then take her back to his place where he could finally erase the memory of Amelia from his bed. He would replace it with Ginger's gorgeous, firm nakedness. Surely, the night couldn't be any better.

Robert pulled his lips from Ginger's and felt someone staring at them. They weren't doing anything differently from the other couples on the dance floor, so he knew that it wasn't that. Still, it was an intense feeling to be watched while being so intimate. He scanned the room until he found the source of the intensity. *Wow!*

True, there was a gorgeous woman wrapped around his waist, but his eyes were locked to the stare of the most beautiful creature he had ever seen. She was a siren with fiery red hair, porcelain skin and the most kissable bow-shaped lips. She was sitting at a table alone, focused completely on what he and Ginger were doing. Her blue dress clung to her in all the right places and rode high on her creamy thighs. Tiny feet were crowned by high, strappy heels that laced up her calves, and Robert instantly got a flash of them resting on his shoulders as she lay beneath him. Dainty fingers ran up and down her bottle of water, and his cock grew harder imaging how those fingers would feel stroking him in the same way. Ginger thought it was in response to what she was doing and turned up her grinding, and his attention was reluctantly drawn back to the blonde on his waist. Ginger closed her eyes and kissed him hungrily, but his eyes flew open and darted back to where the redhead had been watching.

Dammit! She was gone. *She* was the ginger he wanted, but he had to deal with Ginger writhing against his rock-hard erection. Suddenly, feeling like he was carrying more weight than he could manage, Robert spun Ginger around and put her feet back on the floor. The song was over, and he pulled them both back to the bar. Another sultry song began, and he could feel Ginger's hesitation to leave the floor, but he needed to clear his mind and think for a moment. Ginger was doing her best to keep him from the task at hand and whispered naughtily in his right ear. Robert barely heard her because he was vehemently scanning the crowd for his temptress. He needed to find her. He was going to find her. He knew that he was being less than the perfect date, but with the way that woman had blown his mind just by looking at him, he couldn't think about that now. Dammit, where *was* she?

"Hi," a throaty, seductive voice said from his left.

Robert spun around and was face to face with his mystery woman. Ginger clung to him possessively as he felt heavily burdened by the beautiful woman staking her claim.

The woman's eyes softened in response to Ginger's possession. "Easy, Gorgeous, I'm actually here for *both* of you."

Robert's and Ginger's eyes widened in surprise.

"Yes, both of you. You see, I couldn't help notice you when you walked in. You're easily the most beautiful people in here tonight; well, present company excluded, of course." Her eyes roamed up and down their bodies. "And your athleticism on the dance floor was just – wow."

Robert was at a loss for words. He just knew that the night was going to end with him being buried in Ginger. Now, listening to the naughtiness spouting from the sweet, beautiful package standing in front of him, there was a promise of even more than Ginger swallowing him whole. Never could he have imagined *this*. Though he was no stranger to threesomes – a man who looked like he did could have just about anything he wanted – he had never had one with a woman who affected him like this one did.

"Let me buy you both a drink and tell you what I have in mind," the redhead finished. "Oh, and I'm Erica. It's delightful to meet you." She winked a mischievous blue eye and turned to walk away.

Robert looked over at Ginger, who was taking all of this in with curious caution. He asked her permission to proceed, and his date nodded. Relief and excitement flooded him as they followed the sexiest woman he'd ever met to her table.

When they sat down with their drinks, Robert introduced him and Ginger and listened to Erica's proposition. She calmly explained everything in detail and sat back and waited for their response.

"So, we follow you back to your apartment, and we all…" Ginger swallowed, unable to complete her sentence.

"Have hot, fun, sweaty sex, yes!" finished Erica with excitement illuminating her beautiful blue orbs.

"Well, when you put it that way," Robert began and looked over at Ginger.

Ginger did not look amused, and Robert's face fell. He knew that he was manipulating a woman who had been trying to get his attention for well over a month, and part of him felt like an ass doing it. But, then he looked over at Erica. Every part of his body sang when she smiled back. He had to do this, to feel her. Most men viewed a threesome as the Promised Land, but he had been there already. To have a threesome with women who looked like Ginger and Erica would be something else entirely. This was a chance at the Holy Grail! Ginger just *had* to go along with it.

He could tell that she was wavering, so he turned it up a notch. "Ginger, as much as I want this, if it makes you uncomfortable," he punctuated the word 'want' with a growl, "we don't have to." He looked at her with the sincerest stare he could muster, begging her silently to say yes.

Ginger looked at Erica and then at Robert and sighed. "Oh, what the hell; it could be fun!"

Erica clapped her hands and squealed with glee! She just knew that Barbie was going to throw a kink in her plans. She wanted those perfect breasts in her mouth, but she also wanted Robert more than she'd wanted a man since she'd laid her eyes on John.

Robert was fucking gorgeous! The blue in his eyes rivaled hers, and his curly, jet-black hair would be so fun to tangle her fingers in while he feasted on her body. She just bet that his cock would be built just as hard and strong as the rest of him was. If tonight went well, she could see herself playing with him for a very long time. He looked like something that stepped right out of the pages of a magazine.

Or a fairytale.

Erica shut that voice up quickly and replaced it with thoughts of his big hands on her tiny body.

She rubbed her hands together greedily and smiled a hungry smile.

"Shall we?"

She stood and escorted the couple out of the club toward her apartment.

Tonight was certainly turning out better than she'd expected.

CHAPTER 6

Robert had heard of the "Fight or Flight" response, but he'd never seen it in action until tonight.

Erica had explained everything to them in great detail like some rehearsed speech he was certain she had given to many other couples. The more she talked, the wider Ginger's eyes became. She'd explained safewords and limits and then sauntered down the hall to wait on them to make the final decision.

Robert looked hopefully at Ginger.

Ginger looked tentative, but she picked a safeword: Cantaloupe.

Robert laughed. In all of the recent excitement, he'd almost forgotten that he'd told her all about his laughing fit today over dinner. Ginger was definitely a breath of fresh air.

He stood and offered his hand to the buxom blonde. She took it, and he pulled her up into a quick kiss.

"Thank you for this," he said with genuine appreciation.

"Robert, just don't forget to say an extra prayer of thanks tonight. You are a very lucky man!" Ginger teased.

Robert genuinely laughed for the second time today. Things were definitely looking up.

That was, until they opened the door to Erica's playroom.

Erica stood there completely naked. In his wildest dreams, he couldn't have pictured her any more perfectly. Her skin was like fresh cream, and he was parched. Her nipples were small raspberries perched atop large, natural breasts that he couldn't wait to taste. Seeing Erica's heavy, natural, soft breasts, Robert realized that they were much more appealing to him than the firm, silicone ones that Ginger carried. But, in all, it was Erica's hair that caught his attention the most. It was a fiery frame to the most stunning picture ever. He longed to see it spread out underneath her, blue eyes wide and perfect mouth open, as he eased inside of her.

Ginger wasn't as impressed. She looked from Robert to Erica and back and then said the one thing that would put an end to the evening.

"Cantaloupe."

Both Erica and Robert gaped at her.

"What?" Robert did his best not to lose his temper. He wanted this so much, but he quickly realized that it was only Erica he wanted. Ginger was standing in the way of that happening. Still, to Erica, they were a package deal. He needed Ginger to have Erica.

"I thought I could, but I can't," Ginger said. "I'm leaving." She tapped her foot impatiently. "Robert, are you coming?"

"Well, not like he was going to come, but he's definitely leaving with you," Erica petulantly spat while reaching for her robe on the back of the door and shrugging it on. "It's a pity, too. We were going to have a fantastic evening."

Robert couldn't leave it like this. He was intoxicated with Erica, and he had to know what she was like.

"Ginger, honey, are you sure you couldn't try?" Robert all but begged.

Ginger shook her head to reinforce her commitment to leave. "I can't, Robert. This just isn't me."

Robert was not ready to leave. He looked over at Erica. "Give us a moment, please?"

Erica sighed. He really was something, so she did something she didn't normally do. She gave him a second chance.

"Okay. I'll be in here, waiting. Let me know what you decide, but please don't take too long. I get bored quickly." She dropped her robe so that Robert could get a last glimpse of her body and shuffled them out of the room.

Erica picked up her discarded robe and hung it back where it belonged. Fucking spoiled Barbie doll! She had a feeling that the spoiled blonde would get her way. Women who looked like her usually did. It was a shame, too. Robert looked like he could have been a whole lot of fun. Not only was he gorgeous and well-built, but there was something in his eyes that told her that he was funny and smart. She liked funny and smart. But, maybe it was a blessing in disguise. She already had a funny, smart, brick wall in Brock; she didn't need another. But still, there was *something* about Robert that she couldn't put her finger on. Of course, there was also the whole thing about not getting *her* way. There was only enough room in her playroom for one spoiled Princess who always got her way, so it was best that Silicone Barbie chickened out.

Erica sprinted across the room and jumped up in the air, spread her arms and landed in a flop on the cool satin sheets. She giggled as she settled into the bed and reveled in the way the sheets felt against her naked body. She didn't get her way tonight, but there was no reason she couldn't have an orgasm. Looking at Robert handle his date on the dance floor so expertly had gotten Erica's mind wandering, and standing so close to him in the doorway of the room under the scrutiny of his gaze was quite intense.

Erica's hands began to slide down her body. Though it wouldn't be the orgasm she'd planned, an orgasm was still an orgasm, and the night was still young.

CHAPTER 7

Robert stood on the sidewalk and watched as the taxi's taillights disappeared in the darkness. He'd been unable to convince Ginger to go back to Erica's room, so he'd called her a cab instead. She'd looked hurt and disappointed when he closed the car door without sliding in beside her, but he couldn't. There was something tangibly pulling him back inside the apartment, and it was more than just the stunning siren inside. His lower brain was throwing every curse word at him for letting Ginger slip away after longing to be inside of her all day. She would have been his first since She-Who-Shall-Not-Be-Named and would have been a perfect reintroduction to the dating scene. Now, if he couldn't convince Erica to let him back in, he'd have to take matters into his own hands tonight, and that would be a far cry from the ending that he had planned.

He couldn't get back up to Erica's top-floor apartment fast enough. The elevator had been excruciatingly slow, and he'd prayed all the way up that she hadn't locked the door behind him. By a stroke of luck, the knob turned completely as he opened the door.

Robert stepped into the apartment, locked the door behind him and looked around. This woman definitely had money. The apartment was lavishly furnished in dark wood and leather, and the rugs and drapery were all some of the finest he'd ever seen. It was classy and sexy, just like its occupant.

His heart fell as he looked around and didn't see Erica. Surely, she didn't give up that quickly and gone to bed – and certainly not without locking the door! Even in this neighborhood, one of the best and most expensive in town, no one in their right mind would go to bed with their door unlocked. Unless, he thought hopefully, she was waiting on him to come back. That must be it! That *had* to be it! *Please* let that be it!

The rest of the apartment was a blur as Robert sprinted down the hall to the last room and stood a moment before going inside. He had to be right. He closed his eyes and gripped the cold, brass doorknob tightly and then froze.

What was that?

Tiny mewls of pleasure whispered their welcome through the closed door. They danced over his body just like Erica's fingers had stroked her bottle of water in the club. Each one was a melody of longing that harmonized with his desire. He grew hard instantly as the siren sang her song knowing that he was just as doomed as the mythological ships lured by their sweet sound.

Mewls grew to pants, and the pants progressed to deep, throaty moans as he stood there, listening and longing. If he waited any longer, he was going to come with her, though without her. That thought drove him as crazy as her cries. He couldn't stand there any longer and not see the way she looked when she came. Robert knew that she would look glorious, like a supernova heralding the death of one star while birthing millions of others, and, by God, he wouldn't miss it.

Just as her cries began to inch closer to their climax, Robert opened the door, and what he saw was more perfect than anything he'd imagined on the other side of the door.

Erica's creamy legs were spread wide so that he could see the fingers of one hand stroking her perfect, bare, glistening pussy that sat beautifully above her tiny rose-budded ass. Her thigh muscles were clinched with passion, and he knew that she was about to come. She was reclined on a stack of pillows so that he got a great view of her other hand squeezing a nipple harder with each stoke of her lower hand. Her breasts were swollen and heavy, and her nipples were flushed with her desire. Her gorgeous face was contorted for a moment in perfect passion that changed to fury in an instant.

Robert's mouth dried, and his brain had a moment to think *Uh-oh* before the fury was unleashed.

"What the fuck are you doing?"

Erica flew up out of the bed like a tiny missile aimed right at Robert.

He'd never been at a loss for words, not even when he'd seen Amelia naked for the first time, and she had been beautiful. Yet, staring at Erica coming down off a near-orgasm and consumed by blind fury shut his brain completely down. Now *she* was shock and awe!

"Don't just stand there at stare at me like an idiot! Answer me!" she demanded.

Robert blinked, and his communication system came back online.

"I'm sorry, but if you want me to be able to form complete sentences, as much as it pains me to say this, I'm going to need for you to put your robe back on."

Erica stood there contemplating her options. *To clothe or not to clothe?* She looked at the gorgeous man standing there, inches from her, and studied him. There was laughter mixed with fire in his eyes, and his breathing gave away just how close he was to losing all of his carefully contained control. She shifted her weight, and he took a breath. She shifted back to the other foot, and his jaw clinched. Every movement she made, no matter how insignificant, drew a response from his gorgeously-sculpted body. She had her answer.

"No. I don't think I will." She narrowed her eyes in a challenge.

Robert surprised them both by laughing so hard that it filled the entire apartment.

"Suit yourself, Princess. I definitely like the view."

Princess? No one called her 'Princess' but Daddy, the one man who truly loved her. There was no way this infuriating, *stunning,* oaf, *Prince,* of a man was going to call her the same thing.

She crossed her arms under her breasts and made them bounce with her conviction.

"Don't call me 'Princess!'" she spat.

Robert wanted to laugh again, but he didn't want the situation to escalate any further. Doing so would defeat his purpose. He was going to be the one to give Erica the orgasm that his unexpected entrance had denied her. He just needed to calm her down and convince her that it was the perfect way to end their evening, so he raised his hands in surrender.

"Easy," he smiled the smile that usually melted hearts and opened legs. "Can we start over, please?"

"Nice try, Pretty Boy, but I know all the tricks. Your pearly whites won't work on me," Erica argued. Still, his smile *was* nice, and with his arms raised like that, she could easily back him into the St. Andrews Cross directly behind him and have her way with him. Wouldn't that take him down a notch or three? She'd bet he'd never been dominated by a woman before, and she would love to be that woman.

Suddenly, it was all she wanted to do.

Dammit!

Robert faltered a moment. His smile *always* worked. Where was she hiding her kryptonite? He had to find it and get rid of it if he was going get her underneath him, or on top of him or beside him or wherever the hell she wanted to be, just as long as he was inside of her.

His brain scrambled for a change of subject and ran over the course of the evening that led them to this moment. After a moment, he had it. *She'd* invited *him* here! This was *her* idea!

"Look, you obviously wanted me here," he began carefully, "and I want to be here, more than I can put into words."

Erica's eyes narrowed, but her posture softened a little. Taking that as a good sign, he slowly lowered his arms and continued, "Please, let me stay."

There, he said it. She had to let him stay. He didn't know if his legs could physically walk him out of here without experiencing her.

If she were honest with herself, Erica wanted him to stay, but she couldn't let him. She had a strict rule that there were no one-on-ones until she trusted her partner, be it a man or a woman, and even at that, it was rare. She couldn't. Not after her first time. That would *never* happen again. As much as it disappointed her to tell him no, it had to be done.

Robert watched the stunning picture of confliction in front of him. She was silently arguing with herself, and it was the cutest thing he'd ever witnessed. She had to let him stay. He was completely under her spell. He knew that he'd go mad if she made him leave. Then she said the words that would send him on that journey.

"No. You have to go." Erica struggled with the words internally though was pure conviction on the outside.

Robert wasn't so strong, and he didn't care if Erica saw it. He wanted her to know that she affected him, that he wanted her.

"Erica, please," Robert tried to imbue the two words with the longing he felt in that moment.

Erica. The sound of her name coming from him was unlike anything she'd ever heard. It was full of need and longing. It was full of emotion. It broke through her defense. She couldn't believe she was doing this.

She closed her eyes and took a deep breath.

"Okay."

When she opened her eyes to look at Robert, what she saw was a man who looked as if he'd just been given greatest treasure on earth.

Prince Charming, indeed.

Erica felt in her gut that she would be fucked in more than one way by the time the night was over.

Fuck!

CHAPTER 8

Robert fell to his knees at Erica's feet.

She said *yes*.

He would spend every moment she gave him worshiping her and making her happy that she let him stay. No woman had ever had this effect on him before, and he had to find out what it was about her that stripped away his pride and made him happy to see it go.

He looked up at her as his hands started at her ankles and slowly ran up the backs of her legs. They were so soft, so smooth, like silk and satin and everything soft he'd ever felt combined. His blue eyes locked with hers as he bent to run his nose up the inside of her thigh. Robert inhaled deeply when he reached the top.

"So intoxicating," he murmured against her skin.

Erica sighed. Robert had barely touched her, and her skin was alive with an electrical current that she'd only usually felt during the buildup of an orgasm. This was going to be so good – and so *not* at the same time. The part of her brain signaling the four-alarm fire was shut down by the part of her that was relishing the strange way this beautiful man was making her feel. With one mention of her name on his lips, he'd broken her. She'd heard many, many men say her name, plead her name, scream her name, but never had it sounded like Robert had made it sound – like a plea wrapped in a prayer on the most beautiful song. She needed to hear it again.

She wrapped her hands in his curly black mane and pulled his head back. The instant loss of the warmth from his skin and ragged breath left her feeling cold, and she wanted it back, but she had to hear it again. "Say my name."

Robert jerked his head up and locked blue eyes to blue eyes. Erica held her breath and hoped with everything in her that he would say it.

"Erica."

Robert could have been breathing fire when he said her name with the way it felt as it traveled up her stomach and across her chest before it made it to her ears. It burned its way up her and through her.

"Again," she commanded and pulled his hair tighter.

"Erica."

With that, she pulled his head to her core.

"Now," she ordered.

Robert growled and cupped the most perfect clit between his lips. Erica's knees buckled and then tightened to keep her standing. Robert smiled against her soft folds and licked at her juices. He relished the way her body responded to him. He ducked his head to get a better angle, and she spread her legs wider to allow it. He grabbed her hips to hold her in place before stiffening his tongue and plunging it inside as far as he could. Her pussy sucked him in with a force that made him growl again. She wanted him as much as he wanted her. She could say all she wanted with that smart mouth of hers, but her body couldn't lie.

Her salty-sweetness was the most delicious nectar, and he suckled at her like it was life-sustaining, knowing if she stopped him now and sent him away, he would probably die. A little dramatic, maybe, but at this moment, with Erica standing above him riding his face, he believed it. Everything he did tonight had to convince her that she was right to allow him to stay.

Erica was trembling. Thank goodness she was barefoot. There was no way she could have remained standing during this man's skillful onslaught if she'd still had on her stilettoes. Her orgasm was building. She felt it in her stomach, tightening as it made it way torturously through her body, looking for its release. Just another moment more at the mercy of his skillful tongue was all it would take. Almost…

Robert felt the trembling begin, signaling Erica's impending orgasm, but he couldn't let it happen that quickly. No, he wasn't through tasting her. As much as it pained him, he withdrew his tongue from her swollen clit and replaced it with soft kisses.

"Robert!" Erica groaned and almost collapsed.

He answered her groan by scooping her up with her legs around his neck and carrying her to the bed. Her tiny frame was nothing for him to support, and he was extra careful to lay her back. She squealed in shocked delight. Robert took a moment to look up and saw the surprise in her eyes. Her smile coupled with that look hit him right in the chest. He smiled a genuine, warm smile before spreading her pussy wide with his hands and placing soft kisses from bottom to clit.

What the fuck was that? Erica had never felt so free. One minute, she was grounded, getting ready to orgasm, a feeling she knew all too well. The next, she was up in the air, holding onto this man for dear life, yet feeling safe in his grasp. She flew for a moment before being cradled and laid gently in the middle of her bed. Then he smiled at her, the first *real* smile she'd seen all night, and took her breath away. He silenced the alarms ringing in her head by kissing her in her most intimate place over and over again.

Maddening! He was going to drive her mad with the soft kisses. First her clit, and then just a bit lower, lower still, her opening, lower still, just above her ass, her rosebud and then back up again, slowly, excruciatingly slowly. Again! What's that? Teeth?! Nibbling this time. *Holy shit!*

Erica clawed at the sheets beneath her. This man, still fully clothed, was – there was no other word for it – worshiping her pussy. Who the hell was he to have this much willpower? Usually, her conquests had cum multiple times by now, and she was just starting to get off. But this guy…his mouth…can't think…

Robert was painfully hard. His cock bulged against his pants and begged to break free, but his needs could wait. He had the sweetest pussy he'd ever tasted in his mouth, and he was savoring it for as long as he could. He loved the way Erica responded to his tiny bites. Her legs began trembling against his shoulders, and she'd begun breathing harshly.

"Robert, please," she begged.

That's it. God, his name coming from her was like nothing and everything at the same time.

He flattened his tongue against her flesh and licked her harshly.

"Robert, ppplllleeeaaassseee," she begged again.

Fuck! His cock was killing him, and the hunger in her voice stroked it as sure as if it were her hand. If he didn't make her cum quickly, he was going to explode.

Robert buried his face between her lips and found her clit. He slipped two fingers inside her dripping walls and curled them before stroking her and sucking hard on her clit at the same time.

Erica's eyes flew open.

"Shit!" she screamed.

The light was suddenly too bright in the room, and her body was too hot and too tight. Erica exploded. That was the only way she knew to explain the feeling. Her orgasm tore through her and burst through at the same place his mouth connected to her body.

After what seemed like endless moments, Erica's body relaxed, and her soft moans tapered off into soft breaths as Robert lapped up the remnants of her orgasm. He licked her until she stopped pulsing and placed one last, tender kiss on her clit. Erica flinched, and he smiled again.

Robert cocked his head up to look at Erica. "That was to thank you for letting me stay," he said smoothly.

She reached over and grabbed a clean hand towel from the nightstand. She tossed it at Robert and grinned.

"Clean yourself up. It's your turn, Pretty Boy!"

CHAPTER 9

Robert caught the towel in mid-air and did as he was told, though he knew that no amount of wiping would ever erase Erica's sweetness from his memory. He kept his eyes on her as she moved catlike off the bed to stand before him. Everything about her captivated Robert, and he hadn't even felt her bare body against his, tasted her kiss or, hell, even been inside her yet. Surely she was some kind of devil, or a witch, sent to steal his soul, but seeing her standing before him, gloriously naked with flaming curls pouring down her porcelain skin, he knew that he'd gladly give it to her if it meant never having to spend a day without her.

"What to do to you?" Erica's teasing brought him out of his worship, and he shook his head as if to clear some dense fog. "You pleased me so well…" her melodic voice trailed off in mock thought.

Robert could have stared at her all night were it not for the aching in his pants. His cock was the hardest he'd ever known it to be and was demanding to break free of its denim prison.

"Well, I do feel slightly overdressed," he teased back. "You know, a good hostess would do something about that." He was careful not to push too hard, but he loved the natural playfulness between them. It was ...different. It was easy.

Erica motioned for him to put his hands in hers, and he complied without hesitating. His large hands swallowed hers, so petite and dainty, and he was immediately overcome with a need to protect this beautiful woman – whom he'd known only a couple of hours. Had his brain been getting the lion's share of blood flow, he might have felt ridiculous feeling that strongly. However, his brain was starving, and his cock was throbbing, and they both needed him to relieve their urgent states.

Erica couldn't wait to unwrap the gorgeous man standing in front of her. It was like Christmas and her birthday all wrapped up in a blue sweater and jeans. However, she needed to keep control. After all, she called the shots in her playroom, and Pretty Boy here was going to know it. Sure, he had taken her off guard by sweeping her off her feet, literally, and by taking his sweet time making sure she came first, but she couldn't let him know how much his smile – the genuine one he gave her earlier tonight – had disarmed her. Hell, to be honest, she wasn't even letting herself know how much.

To keep her mind on the task at hand, Erica studied each muscle as she revealed it while pulling the soft, blue sweater over Robert's finely kept torso. She had to tip-toe in order to get it over his mane of black curls after he raised his arms in compliance.

Erica stepped back and admired her handiwork. Damn, he was perfect – on the outside, anyway. There was a dusting of black curls across his muscular chest that she couldn't wait to run her hands through, but first thing's first: he had to lose the pants. At the thought of removing her conquest's pants, she started to salivate, and then Erica knew exactly how she was going to repay him for his attentiveness.

The red-headed temptress in front of him dropped to her knees, and Robert could barely control himself. He watched her tiny fingers deftly unfasten his belt and free him from his button and zipper in record time. He chuckled softly as her eyes darted up to his in a challenge. Not wanting to distract her from her task, he simply smiled and nodded his acquiescence. She went back to her task and painstakingly slowly slid his jeans and boxers down to his ankles at once, letting his erection bounce with its freedom.

"Not bad, Pretty Boy. Not bad at all," Erica smiled at him appreciatively. "Now step."

Brain function being limited, it took a moment for Robert to realize that she meant to step out of his pants, but he did so quickly.

"Good, Boy. Now sit," she commanded softly while staring into his eyes.

The air was charging between the two as Robert slowly eased into a sitting position on the edge of the bed. The energy was palpable. *Surely she had to feel it, too*, Robert thought as he watched her lick her lips while she languidly shifted position and began to kneel.

Oh, her mouth was going to be heaven!

Suddenly, Robert stopped Erica mid-kneel. She looked up at him, and her beautiful face was marred with confusion – and maybe a little hurt, he thought. His brain and his cock screamed at him in unison, *What the fuck are you doing?!?!*

He couldn't let her think that he didn't want her because heaven knows she was all he wanted in that very moment and for all the foreseeable moments to come, but he was overwhelmed with the need to kiss the lips she just moistened with her tongue.

"I just have to…" Robert tried to explain with his words to erase the hint of pain on Erica's face, but he could tell that his words weren't working. He pulled her up gently by her face and crashed his lips into hers.

Erica was still reeling from the rejection of not being able to give Robert the best blow job he'd ever had when, suddenly, his lips were on hers in a frantic kiss. His lips betrayed his desire for her, and the sting of perceived rejection was soothed by the warmth of his kisses. The taste of her desire on his soft lips brought out the animal in Erica, and soon her urgency was meeting his. Their tongues tangled and licked, frolicking in new-found desire.

Robert's arms circled Erica's waist and pulled her closer to him, and she gladly went. As their bodies became closer, their kisses slowed from urgent need to simmering lust. Her whole body was aware of every breath this beautiful man took, and she knew that she had to be careful. Men like him weren't meant for women like her, even though in this one moment, she could let herself believe in fairytales. After all, everything he'd done so far tonight had been

Prince Charming and a Knight in Shining Armor all rolled into one, and, after all, his kisses were so good. Erica squealed to herself when he bit her bottom lip and sucked it into his mouth to massage it with his tongue. Yes, she would let herself have tonight.

Robert ran his hands from Erica's tiny waist and down her perfectly-round bottom, down her thighs and scooped her up to sit on his lap. Her blue eyes opened wide with surprise as he positioned himself as her mount. Erica closed her eyes in preparation of his penetration. Still, after all these years, the anticipation of the first thrust made her flinch even though the physical pain was long gone. She supposed it would always be that way.

"Open your eyes," Robert held her securely just above the tip of his erection while his body shook in barely-contained restraint.

Erica's eyes flew open in response to his command.

"Keep them open," he commanded again.

Her need for him triumphed over her smart mouth, and she locked her eyes to his. Then she was being lowered onto him so that he was slowly pushing her apart. Her instinct was to throw her head back and give him an appreciative moan, but that seemed too theatrical for this moment. It was unlike anything she'd ever known.

This strong, gorgeous man was being gentle with her, savoring her and making her watch. She simply couldn't look away. This was the sweetest possession she'd ever known.

Robert was going to come apart at the seams. Though his cock was screaming to be inside of Erica, he made himself savor each inch of this beautiful woman on his lap as he slid her slowly onto him.

The command to have her look at him took him by surprise. He'd never done that before, but he had been haunted with thoughts of Amelia thinking of her husband while they'd made love, and he would not make that mistake again. Erica was going to know who was fucking her – *making love to her* his mind corrected. Robert shook his head to rid himself of thoughts of Amelia and love and focused on the feeling of Erica's body enveloping his in her velvet embrace.

Her blue eyes heated the deeper he got, and when she had engulfed his entire length inside of her, Robert kissed her again, deeply and softly. She tried to move, but his hands locked down on her hips and held her in place. He needed some time to acclimate to the paradise he was in before her next move made him come completely undone.

Erica's brain was fried! She tried to give this man a blowjob, and he stopped her for a kiss. She tried to ride the massive cock he slipped inside of her *without her flinching!*, a thought that her brain would catalog for her next visit with Dr. Boyd, for sure. Yet he held her still, though instead of frustration, she felt…full. She wrapped her spindly fingers in his hair and met his kisses with vigor. She loved the way the curls on his chest felt on her breasts as he pulled her tighter to him. With her legs wrapped around Robert's waist and captured inside his strong arms, Erica felt something that she'd never felt before – totally and completely *safe*. With that security, Erica took some control back from her lover and started moving up and down, slowly. Erica pulled back just enough to let him know that she planned to honor his command and locked her stare to the liquid sapphire of his eyes.

Robert's hands hungrily roamed her body and branded each place they touched as his. When he took her breasts in his massive hands and squeezed, Erica felt the connection all the way to her core. As she rode him toward his climax, he kissed every part of her body he could reach: her lips, her chin, her neck. The fingers of one hand pinched her nipple while the fingers of the other hand threatened to bruise her hip, they held her so hard. Still, she couldn't get enough of this feeling, of this man beneath her who was lost in her. With his head buried in her neck, she closed her eyes for the first time since his command to open them and gave herself over to being loved.

Robert couldn't get enough of the beautiful woman on his lap. Her kisses urged him onward. The sweat on her body tasted like salted heaven, and the sounds she made when he took her nipples between his teeth vibrated to his core. He wanted to kiss every inch of her, to consume every inch of her. Being inside of her was his new favorite place, and he never wanted to leave. If he lived a thousand lifetimes, he could never get enough of this woman.

Erica felt her insides tightening with the familiar orgasmic pull. Every thrust of Robert's hard cock sent her closer to igniting, and she needed to come with him inside of her. She wanted to feel her pussy's walls spasm around his thickness. The thought made her move faster.

Robert growled and grabbed a fistful of Erica's flaming red hair and pulled her head back. In silent affirmation, she opened her eyes and watched him watch her as her orgasm exploded around him. She rocked and screamed as her body gave way and let the flames from her orgasm consume her completely, never once breaking eye contact with the source of her pleasure in the most intimate moment of her life.

At Erica's eruption, Robert lost his control and let the spasms from her walls massage his shaft to his climax. His voice joined in harmony with hers as the glory of their orgasms washed over him. Seeing her come undone because of him was more than he could process, but he felt it in places no one had ever touched. As he watched the heat from her orgasm leave her eyes, he could tell that Erica had felt something, too.

CHAPTER 10

Robert lay there wide-awake in the early hours of the morning holding Erica as she softly snored in deep sleep. He couldn't believe the turn his evening had taken. What should have been a fun, acrobatic one-night stand with Ginger had turned into one of the most moving nights of his life with the siren sleeping safely in his arms. Surely, she had to have felt something, too. It couldn't have been all him. He was going to have to think through some things. However, all he knew in this moment – this perfect moment – was that he would never be able to get his fill of this woman, but he'd spend his whole life trying, if she'd let him.

Erica stirred and snuggled closer, and Robert tightened his arms around her. *So tiny*, he thought. How could someone so tiny cause such a tremendous upheaval in his soul? He thought back to the flare of her temper when he first opened the door and caught her masturbating. She was so angry! But, aside from the anger, there was passion and fire. Her red hair was certainly aptly colored.

The contrast between Erica and Amelia was striking. Where Amelia was warm and comfortable, Erica was flagrant and unpredictable. He'd thought that making love to Amelia had been the way that love was supposed to feel, but there had definitely been something missing, although he hadn't realized that at the time. That something-missing element fell into place last night when he'd finally nestled into Erica and held her still. It was as if something had clicked into place, and that something was all-encompassing.

Sitting there, locked in the most intimate embrace with Erica, feeling her breathe and adjust to him, feeling her welcome him, filled Robert with a sense of adventure, a feeling of soaring, and at the same time, a sense that he was finally – *home*. That was it. Staring into her wide, burning blue eyes, he'd found his home. Every move, every kiss, everything that had followed that evening had been him trying to make her feel it, too. And she had. For his sake, she had to. He'd nearly lost all pride since the debacle with Amelia. He'd be ruined if he couldn't convince Erica to let him stay.

Yes, he knew this was all absurd. This hot, sex fiend picked him and Ginger up in a club to have a threesome, and, less than eight hours later, he's seeing happily-ever-after as she's sleeping in his arms. His MAN CARD would be revoked for sure, but he couldn't help it. All he knew was how he'd felt from the moment he'd felt her staring at him across the dance floor.

Robert looked down at the beautiful creature sleeping in his arms and pulled her even tighter, as if trying to imprint her body on his and his on hers. Erica sighed sleepily against his chest, and his heart leapt. He was definitely a goner and would happily hand over his MAN CARD to anyone with the guts to ask for it if it meant getting to call Erica his forever home.

Flashes from the night before ran through Erica's brain as she swam up out of one of the best nights of sleep she'd ever had. Her body was deliciously sore as wakefulness invaded her muscles. She sighed contentedly as she snuggled her tiny frame into the wall of muscle that was her pillow.

In the minutes between peaceful sleep and full consciousness, Erica was free to fantasize. She could allow the honesty to wash over her and admit that last night with Robert was much more than she'd ever experienced – had ever hoped to experience. No one had ever made love to her before. She'd been fucked, sucked and spanked, and it had all be fun. *Most of it*, her brain reminded her that honesty was prevailing in her current state. *Fine, most of it*, Erica conceded and snuggled closer to the warmth beside her.

She knew that women like her didn't get their happily-ever-after, but she'd settle for happily-in-the-moment. She inhaled and savored the wonderful man-smell coming from Robert. It was better than any of the expensive perfumes on her vanity, more decadent than the smell of her favorite Parisian bakery with the freshest croissants, even better than – dare she say it – coffee! Erica giggled to herself as she imagined telling Robert that she liked him better than coffee.

What was she thinking? She couldn't let herself get carried away on this train of thought. She'd picked up Robert and Silicone Barbie at the club last night and brought them back here for sex. Period. Sure, he'd disarmed her and convinced her to let him stay and break her No. 1 rule – no one-on-one until she trusted the person. And yes, he'd taken her completely off guard by making sure that she'd come – TWICE – before he'd found his release. And, definitely, he'd felt amazing buried inside of her, like a second helping of ooey-gooey dessert while sitting in a rocking chair on the porch during an autumn Sunday afternoon. But, that's where she would have to leave it, at the bottom of the empty bowl in the vacated rocking chair. There was no way that she could have anything more with Robert, so there was no use fantasizing any longer.

Erica stretched, enjoying the sting in her muscles, and opened her sleepy blue eyes. Part of her was hoping that Robert was still asleep so that she could sneak away and grab a shower, putting some space between her and her temptation. No such luck. There he was, wide awake and looking at her with a gaze that would melt the ooey-gooey dessert from her early-morning fantasy.

"Good morning, Princess," his voice poured the chocolate sauce on her dessert, and her insides clinched. Still, she was going to have to put an end to the "Princess" thing.

She narrowed her eyes at the most charming man she'd ever met. "I told you…" she began.

"I know, only your Daddy calls you 'Princess.' I'm sorry," Robert offered genuinely. "It's just a fitting nickname for you."

Erica sat up, and the red satin sheet pooled down around her waist, exposing her breasts, heavy with her morning fantasy. Was he making fun of her?

"Now, what is that supposed to mean?" her temper flared behind her eyes.

The alarms began to sound in Robert's head, and he knew that he needed to disarm her quickly. This was *not* going the way he wanted it to.

"Nothing," he searched for the right words to convey how he was feeling. "It's just that, lying here with you makes me feel like a king. 'Queen' would be a better name for you, I guess, but it doesn't have the same ring to it as 'Princess.'"

Robert searched her face for some hint that she'd felt his sincerity. Her blue eyes started to soften, and her perfect bow-like mouth turned up at the corners into a sly smile. He relaxed a little and allowed his gaze to keep going down her dainty chin and the feminine slope of her neck. His breath caught when he got to her breasts. They were perfect, though how such a tiny frame supported such large, natural breasts was beyond him. They were milky white with the most perfect rose-colored areolas and tiny pink nipples. Remembering the way they felt pressed up against him last night and the way they tasted in his mouth brought his attention to his morning erection, already awake from holding Erica as she slept. Now, it was almost painful.

Erica's musical giggle brought his eyes back up to hers. She was brimming over with mischief, and Robert swore that he'd never seen a more beautiful sight. She was a queen who deserved his loyalty, a jewel he wanted to shine and protect and the vision of the most beautiful witch putting him deeper under her spell.

"A queen, you say?" Erica began and slid out of bed, pulling the red satin top sheet with her. When she spun to face Robert, she stood there with it gathered in one hand at her throat while the rest of the rich fabric flowed down around her like a queen's coronation robe. With her untamed mess of waist-length flaming curls and the rich red satin flowing down her ivory skin, she looked like a porcelain deity ready to be worshiped by her hedonistic followers, of which Robert was her most fervent.

Robert swallowed hard. "Not 'a' queen," he leveled his stare so that she knew he was serious. With all sincerity, he finished, "*My* queen."

What had started as a simple, funny role-playing session for Erica turned serious all too quickly. She was stunned with how the tiny word 'my' sounded so huge when spoken by Robert. This beautiful, naked man was suddenly at her feet kissing each one. Feet were not sexy, but, somehow, he made them burn all the way to her core. He placed little kisses all the way up both of her legs that reminded her of the kisses he placed on her clit last night, and Erica's knees almost betrayed her. While his kisses traced the front of her legs, his strong hands lit a fire up the back of them. Erica clenched when he reached the top of her thighs and anticipated his next kiss. Yet, instead of the assault on her clit that she had anticipated, she was suddenly scooped up in his arms with her legs wrapped around his waist. She gasped and released the makeshift cape so that her hands could hold tight to Robert.

The hard wall was at Erica's back imprisoning her between it and Robert's hard chest. She was poised just above the tip of his steel cock with no escape. Yet, instead of the harsh penetration she expected, he lowered her with the same slow, deliberate pace as he had the night before, never letting his eyes leave hers. His strong hands supported her from the bottom and helped her move. The hard chest that imprisoned her softened against her body as his lips found hers.

Erica was floating somewhere between fantasy and real life as he made love to her against the wall of her playroom. Robert's kisses grew more urgent as he rocked into her. The friction was building, and she was soon to be another inferno because of this man. She didn't care if she'd burn. The way he kissed her while he held her tight and made love to her in this moment was worth any amount of fiery torment.

Erica's body tightened once more before exploding. Still, Robert never broke his kiss and swallowed every moan of her orgasm as he pushed further into her body chasing his own satisfaction. As he poured into her, Erica swallowed his in return, in what was single-handedly the most intimate moment that she'd ever experienced. Her eyes threatened tears as he lowered both of their bodies to the floor. Thankfully, he was still kissing her so that she could will the tears to stop.

Robert couldn't bear to break either the kiss or to leave the comfort of Erica's body, so he held both fast as he lowered them to the floor. Her little frame was so easy to support as he guided her below him, but he knew he had to be careful as he lowered his weight on top of her. The last thing he wanted to do was hurt her in any way.

A sniffle made Robert break his kiss.

"Are you okay?" Robert's eyes darted from her head, down her beautiful body to her perfect toes and back up again. He began to stiffen again. "I didn't hurt you; did I?"

Erica smiled and wiped at her eyes. *Dammit!* "No, Pretty Boy. Allergies. That's all."

"Are you sure?" It didn't look like allergies to him, but what did he know? He was in marketing, not med school.

"Yes, I'm sure," Erica answered. "Now, if you'll politely move, I'd like to get up now." Erica lied. There was nowhere else she wanted to be at this very moment, but she couldn't let him know that. She needed to put some space between her and Robert immediately if she was to salvage anything of the wall remaining around her heart.

It was Robert's turn to tease. "Well, *I'm* up, so I'm moving," he looked down at her with a grin that would make even the Devil sell his soul and pushed back inside of her.

Erica couldn't hold back her surprise. "Wow!" Robert hit her deep and made everything inside her vibrate.

"I like 'wow,'" he genuinely laughed, and she joined in.

"Well then, you're going to love this," Erica said and surprised Robert by using his body as leverage while flipping over underneath him.

"Oh, you witchy woman," Robert growled in her ear.

It was Erica's turn to laugh as Robert sat up on his knees and lifted her bottom by her hips. She flipped her hair back so that it landed at the small of her back, twitched her hips and was immediately rewarded by his gasp.

"How did I miss such a perfect ass, Princess?"

Erica savored the head of his penis poised at her opening and dipped her back as he slid inside, parting her wide. Goosebumps broke out on her entire body as he slowly moved in and out of her, driving her mad. Surely, he would speed up. Doggy style was meant for fucking, after all.

"Do you have any other speed," Erica bit out between languid thrusts.

"Do I?" Thrust. "Let's see." Harder thrust. "What about." Slow thrust. "This," Robert growled and pulled Erica's arms up by the wrists while he pounded his steel into her.

Erica closed her eyes and relished the sensation of being taken by a man she knew would protect her and keep her safe. She allowed her body to respond to his control as she called out his name over and over. Another orgasm threatened to rip through her as he pounded into her fast and hard.

"Robert, fuck!" Erica screamed as she came again, this time spouting every profanity she'd ever heard.

"Fuck!" Robert's cry joined hers as his climax ripped through him.

His body collapsed on top of hers, and they lay there in a panting, sweaty mess. Robert moved her hair to reveal exposed flesh and placed his famous little kisses on the back of her neck and across her shoulder. Erica tensed, not knowing what she hoped for more: a declaration of some intense feeling or a hasty goodbye.

Robert bit into her shoulder and then leaned in to her ear. The anticipation was killing her slowly from the inside out.

"And now," Robert kissed her ear lobe.

Erica held her breath.

"Pancakes!" Robert leapt up and reached for her hand.

Erica released her breath. Relief washed over her with his simple, easy request. Luckily she'd stocked her kitchen. Pancakes were exactly what she needed.

"Pancakes," Erica echoed her reply and put her hand in his.

Robert's answering smile melted her insides like the syrup she intended to drench her pancakes in.

"But first, a shower," she said.

"Ladies first," Robert replied. "I'll find my way through your kitchen."

Erica stood back and looked Robert up and down before giving him a curious smile.

"What?" Robert asked in answer to her questioning smile.

Erica shook her head and was overcome with a moment of honesty.

"You look like something that stepped right out of a fairytale, fuck like a porn star and offer to cook me breakfast after serving me back-to-back orgasms…and they say that chivalry is dead," Erica winked and sauntered down the hall with Robert's heart.

CHAPTER 11

Erica shut the door to the bathroom and fell against it. She was finally free to catch the breath she had been holding in a meditative effort to control the gallop of her heart in her chest as she walked away from Robert. She stared at her reflection in the mirror. She didn't look any differently than she did before her trip to the club last night. Her hair was just as unruly; her eyes just as blue. But her lips – there was certainly a change there. They were plumper than before, surely the result of his refusal to stop kissing her.

So, what the hell had happened?

A hot shower; that's what she needed. A hot shower was the answer for everything in this moment. Erica stepped under the steaming water and groaned as the first waves washed down her body. She tilted her head under the cascading heat and closed her eyes as the water rinsed away the aching in her muscles. As she lathered her red mane with a generous amount of shampoo, she wondered how life could change in the span of a few short hours.

Before going to the club last night, she'd known exactly who she was and what to expect out of life. Not only had she known, but she had been content with that knowledge. Before laying her eyes on Robert, she'd known what to expect out of men – and women, for that matter. There might be a little variation between the lot of them, but they always behaved the same in the end. Her life was cruising right along with no complications. She enjoyed her playthings and sent them away in the morning, only keeping her favorites to play with in her Playhouse, like life-size toys.

Then *he* had to walk into the club right when she was getting ready to leave. Had she left just a few minutes sooner, she would never have invited him back to her apartment. *And never had had the best night of your life!* Ugh! Erica scrubbed her scalp extra hard, trying to shut off her brain from screaming the truth that her heart felt.

In all truth, it had, indeed, been the best night of her life. Within the four walls of her playroom – a room that had seen its fair share of fetishes, debauchery and kink –, Erica had discovered what it felt like to be loved, and it had been indescribably delicious! It also wasn't fair. Having never felt loved before, she hadn't known what she was missing. Ignorance truly was bliss. But now, *dammit*! She should definitely be careful what she wished for. This was karmic justice for longing for John Foster and fantasizing about rolling around with him, being looked at and touched the way he had done to his wife, for making a play for him when they had visited her Playhouse. Never in her wildest imaginings did she ever think it would feel like this, and it gave her a greater appreciation for Amelia's reaction to her kissing John that fateful evening. Surely, if Robert was hers and someone else had made a play for him, Erica would have reacted the same way. Oh, how she hated contrition!

Erica rinsed her locks and applied her conditioner. If Robert were hers…she couldn't even allow herself to begin thinking that way. She was definitely damaged, a whole mess of issues wrapped in a pretty package. A man like Robert, so loving and gentle, didn't deserve her concentrated crazy. He was surely rethinking breakfast and was probably out the door before she stepped into the shower. So, she would have to chalk last night and this morning up to experience.

After all, it wasn't often that a woman with her appetites experienced something new.

She'd imagined what a night like last night would have been like with John many times, but she had had nothing to compare it to. She couldn't have known how beautiful – truly beautiful – she would feel being worshiped by a man. She couldn't have known how safe she would feel alone with him, wrapped in his arms. Though she had had many men inside of her, she couldn't have known the feeling of being truly complete. But now, after spending a night with Robert, she knew, and she would be forever changed.

Erica finished her shower and stepped out to wrap herself and her hair into luxury towels and then wiped the fog from the mirror. She brushed her teeth and towel-dried her hair before grabbing the robe off the back of the bathroom door.

Surely he should be gone by now. Though the thought both saddened her and filled her with relief at the same time, her stomach won the battle as it demanded the fulfillment of the promise of pancakes. She would do a cursory check of the apartment first, just to be sure that she was right, and then get dressed and go out for the biggest stack of pancakes she could buy. Maybe she'd even invite Brock.

Robert stood at the stove, taking up the last of the pancakes and bacon from the griddle when he heard the bathroom door open. He'd refused to let himself dwell over the what-ifs while he was making breakfast so that he didn't burn anything. The last thing he needed to do while setting out on his quest to woo Erica was to burn down her kitchen.

"Oh, my God, that's bacon!" Erica exclaimed from down the hall. The hunger in her voice was evident.

"I know I just mentioned pancakes, but I hope you don't mind that I added bacon," Robert answered innocently.

"Are you kidding? Bacon makes everything better!" Erica hurried down the hall to the kitchen and scooped up a piece to devour before Robert could find the plates in the cupboard.

He turned to look at the beauty in front of him.

"I don't know if it makes everything *better*; right here, right now, you're kinda hard to improve upon." His honesty surprised him, but at this point, he didn't have much to lose. If he was going to make Erica his, then he couldn't pull any punches now.

"Pretty Boy, you keep getting better and better," Erica teased as she grabbed another piece of bacon. "But right now, you need to sit down and eat if you plan to have any breakfast. I'm starving."

Robert laughed and shook his head while filling their plates with food. Coffee and juice were already on the table, and Erica began indulging in the sweet caffeine as she waited on her breakfast. Though coffee was heavenly, she definitely liked Robert more and grinned at the thought.

"What?" Robert asked.

"Nothing," Erica blushed at being caught in her private musing.

"No, you can't look that adorable, grin that sinfully and say 'nothing,'" Robert fired back.

Certainly not wanting to reveal her hand, Erica tried diversion instead.

"You look rather comfortable in my kitchen, you know," she said as Robert placed a plate full of pancakes and a saucer of bacon in front of her. The two pieces of bacon she'd snatched earlier had only made her hungrier, and she couldn't wait to dive into the fluffy pancakes. She reached for the butter and syrup and began prepping her breakfast for her devouring.

"If you've been in one kitchen, you've been in them all, really. I'm just glad you had all of the ingredients for me to make us breakfast. I worked up quite an appetite, thanks to you." Robert put his first forkful of pancakes in his mouth and began eating.

"Oh, my god! These are delicious!" Erica closed her eyes and groaned.

Robert adjusted in his seat. Never had pancakes been so sexy!

"I'm glad you like them."

"What's your secret? My pancakes are good, but these are fantastic!"

"Now, if I told you that, I'd have to kill you," Robert winked at Erica good-naturedly over the breakfast table.

Erica stuck her tongue out at Robert in mock petulance.

"No, seriously. Please?"

"Well, since you said 'please,'" Robert began. "I added a little vanilla to the batter. My mom taught me that trick."

"Remind me to thank your mom!" Erica smiled and then shifted uncomfortably with the implications of her remark.

Robert noticed her discomfort and changed the subject.

"You have a pretty stocked pantry. Do you like to cook?" he asked with genuine inquisitiveness.

Relieved to have something else to talk about other than meeting his mom, Erica replied, "Actually, yes, and I'm pretty good at it, too. I have varied appetites, in all things."

"I'll bet you do," Robert smirked. "Now, eat up so we can get going."

Erica's fork paused just before her mouth.

"Get going? Where are *we* going?"

"Well, Princess, you've had your shower, and I'm sure a massive closet of clean clothes is waiting for you behind one of those doors. I, on the other hand, am at a disadvantage, as all of my clean clothes are across town in *my* closet in *my* apartment."

"And you think I'm going with you, to your apartment," Erica narrowed her eyes and lowered her fork.

Robert answered matter-of-factly, "Absolutely. After last night and this morning, do you really think I can walk away from you now? Now, eat up before your breakfast gets cold."

Erica sat there dumbfounded. She had been sure he would run, but here he sat across from her having a delicious breakfast that he'd made for them and planned to spend the day with her. She knew she should make him leave now because when he ran later, she knew she would truly hurt, but she couldn't make herself. She'd never been good at denying herself anything she desired, so why should she start now? What was a little heartache, anyway?

She picked up her fork and enjoyed the rest of her breakfast in comfortable silence with the handsome man across from her and actually looked forward to the day ahead.

CHAPTER 12

Erica marveled at the ease of their conversation as they strolled down the street hand-in-hand. Robert had spent most of the short walk from her apartment to the parking lot at the club to retrieve his car talking about his job in marketing. The creative type fit him, she decided, as she studied the way the muscles in his jaw moved as he spoke. She loved that, too, she decided.

Just as she was settling into a comfortable stride with her handsome escort, Robert stopped and stood still. His eyes became filled with what Erica had only heard described as worship, and he broke out into that genuine smile that rivaled the ones he had given her since last night. The unfamiliar finger of jealousy crept up her spine thinking of whatever woman brought out that reaction in Robert. She knew that she had no right to succumb to the green venom, but she had. Before opening her mouth to speak, she followed his gaze.

Really?

Oh, he's such a guy!

"Your *car*, I presume," she snarked.

Robert looked down at her in amusement. "If you must call her a 'car,' then yes, she is my *car*." He filled the last word with all of the affection a man could hold for an inanimate object. "She is…"

"A 1967 Camaro – Year One; yeah, I know," Erica completed his sentence for him.

Robert was stunned. He looked over at Erica in awe. How could this pint-size powerhouse Princess, who was surely spoiled on chauffeurs and Town Cars know about his prized possession?

Erica grinned. "So, there's more to me than palaces and ponies; huh?"

Robert gave her his smile. "How…"

"…do I know what kind of car this is?" Erica again finished his sentence. "Simple, really, I love cars. I actually learned to drive in a 1969 Camaro Rally Sport. It was green with yellow racing stripes. Oh, she was gorgeous. She was Daddy's."

Robert watched as Erica's eyes followed some distant memory

down an old dirt road before coming back to the present. She was full of surprises, and he couldn't wait to uncover them all.

"So, you like her?" Robert cautiously asked. Not that it would matter if she did or didn't because he was determined to make Erica a part of his life, but it would be so much easier if she didn't whine about every minute he spent detailing his car.

Erica could tell that Robert was very proud of and quite fond of the beauty in the parking spot, but she'd make him agonize over her answer while she inspected the machine. She was a very beautiful car; Robert obviously cared for her. She had a beautiful true blue exterior and had shining chrome trim. Looking through the windows, she could see impeccable black leather interior and could almost imagine how it smelled. Erica closed her eyes and remembered back to her Daddy's Camaro and the way that smell always brought her back to driving down dirt roads with the windows down and the radio blaring. When she opened them, she could tell that Robert was obviously waiting on an answer. It was almost as painful as watching him wait on her to tell him that he could stay after Ginger walked out on their threesome. *Almost.*

Erica ran her fingers sensuously down the hood and looked at

Robert. The sunlight from the morning's sun cast a blazing halo around her face, and Robert's Adam's apple leapt into his throat.

"I absolutely…" Erica paused for effect, "Love her!"

Robert closed the space between himself and his two favorite women in one long stride and scooped Erica up into his arms.

"You love torturing me; don't you?" he said playfully.

"You haven't seen torture yet. I can be Mistress Erica and show you," Erica winked.

Robert's entire body tingled at the promise in her teasing and was overcome with the need to kiss her.

And so, he did.

He lowered Erica to her feet, pressed her body up against the passenger window of his beloved car and covered her mouth with his. The autumn day was unfurling around them, encouraging the playfulness in their banter and in their kiss. Erica giggled and sighed musically as a group of leaves danced their way across the parking lot, caught in the light morning breeze, and, to Robert, nothing seemed more perfect.

Erica relished the feel of Robert's body pressed up against hers. The warm automotive steel was at her back, and Robert's denim-sheathed steel was pressing her further into it as his kisses took her to a very happy place. Being overtaken by his kisses in the crisp fall air made her giggle with a carefree spirit that was not known to her. She was usually on high alert, tense with worry or making deals and helping novice men and women pick their safe words. This was just so – *normal*. *Normal*. Even the word sounded funny bouncing around in her head, and that thought made Erica giggle again.

Robert groaned. He wanted something he had never wanted before. He wanted Erica *in* his car, *on* his car; hell, anywhere *near* his car would do. But, he couldn't. Not here, and certainly not in the bright light of morning, so he did the only thing he could do and reluctantly ended their kiss.

Erica looked as if she were going to pout, but Robert quelled her tantrum.

"If we are going to get anywhere today, I have to take my lips off yours. I need a shower and clean clothes, and to get to my apartment, I need you to get in the car."

Erica smiled up at him.

"Why didn't you just say so?" she teased.

Robert laughed and opened her car door to escort her to her seat.

It was a simple gesture, but it was one Erica was not used to at all. She never got into a car with anyone other than her car service – not even Brock, and he was a trusted police detective. Yet, here she was, letting this gorgeous man disarm her completely.

She watched as Robert walked around and opened his door. His agile body slipped easily into the driver's seat, and her body was suddenly all too aware of the close quarters and the heat between them. Her core tightened as she let her eyes roam over his torso and down his strong thighs as his nimble hands buckled his seat belt.

"Buckle up, Princess," Robert brought her out of her appreciation, and she obeyed.

Robert started the car and listened for a moment in appreciation. The throaty rumble from the engine vibrated his body as he revved the motor for more effect.

The vibration from the car was all Erica needed to send her into hypersensitivity after her silent appreciation of Robert's body. The loose, green dress she had chosen for the day was suddenly too tight, and the air was too warm. She was in hell with this heavenly man.

Robert put the straight shift into first gear and expertly pulled out of the parking spot that had been the car's home for the night. Erica trained her eyes on the asphalt in front of her to distract her from the sexy thoughts that seeing Robert's large, skillful hands expertly handle the gear shift delivered.

Oh, Pretty Boy, I'm in so much trouble, she thought to herself and settled in for the ride to the undisclosed location of his apartment.

CHAPTER 13

Erica stood in the middle of the spacious living room of Robert's apartment and took it all in. She wasn't sure what she expected, but it wasn't this. It really was a beautiful space. There was bright, natural light filtering in from the windows that highlighted the natural coloring of the wood floors. The décor was light wood and brushed metal, giving the whole space an expensive, yet relaxing feel. A muted, almost smoky blue couch dominated the living room space, which must have been comfortable because she could tell from the rumpled sheets and bed pillows that it had recently been someone's bed.

Erica walked over and picked up an end of the sheet, the finger of jealousy tickling her spine.

"Recent guest?" she asked and watched as Robert's body tensed.

His jaw clenched tight, and he dropped his eyes to the floor. Erica watched as his Adam's apple bobbed with a slow swallow as he obviously contemplated how to answer.

Silence stretched between them, and, for the first time since laying eyes on Robert in the club, she felt awkward. Though she wasn't one to bite her tongue when she wanted to know something, seeing the pain rip across Robert's handsome features made her wish she could take her question back.

Robert closed his eyes and felt the familiar feeling of Amelia's ghost wrap around his body as he had so many times since their night together. He'd tried to sleep in his bed many nights since then, but her dark eyes and chocolate-hued hair haunted it. The couch had been his only refuge. Still, she'd found her way out here, too, but how could he say that to Erica?

He opened his eyes and looked over to where she stood, a vision of bright-red hair decked out in a jade dress. She was such a vivid contrast to the brightness of his apartment. She was bold. She was beautiful. As he stood there taking her in, Robert was filled with something he hadn't felt since Amelia didn't return to him – hope.

He could see the concern in Erica's face, and he wanted to take it away from her immediately. Such a beautiful creature should never have concern mar their face.

Robert swallowed one more time and found his voice.

"No. No guest," he said and offered her a smile that did not quite touch his eyes as did the others he'd given her since they'd met.

Erica finally let go of the end of the sheet and let it fall back to its resting place.

"Oh," was her only reply. The tickling touch of jealousy's finer changed to a fist that wrapped around her stomach.

Robert knew that he had to change the subject before the awkwardness pushed them too far apart. After all, they'd only met last night, and since he felt her eyes on him, all he'd wanted was to keep her close. He would not push her away.

"It's a long story, one better told over shots of Patron and not on a full stomach,"

he smiled again. This time, it was genuine.

Erica shifted. "Look, you don't have to say anything."

"And I won't…at least not until *after* I shower." Robert closed the gap between them and took Erica in his arms. "I'm sorry. I went somewhere I never want to be again. Thank you for pulling me out of it. I'm going to jump in the shower. Please feel free to look around and make yourself at home."

Robert kissed her on her forehead as if she were a precious treasure, and Erica melted on the inside, releasing jealousy's grip. She stood frozen in place and watched as he disappeared down the hall.

How could he be real? Maybe he's not. Maybe the whole night and morning had been one messed-up dream, the product of some bad seafood or some curdled cream in her coffee. Yet, here she stood in the beautiful apartment of the most beautiful man she'd ever met. Not only was he beautiful on the outside, but she was starting to see that he also had a beautiful heart, and someone had been careless with it. Someone had broken it. The thought of Robert being hurt both saddened and angered Erica, taking her by surprise. Sure, she had feelings, but she had worked long and hard to bury them and harden herself from anyone knowing that she was anything more than shallow and cold. That way, she could protect herself from the same hurt she saw in Robert moments ago. Yet in a short 24 hours, Pretty Boy had found his way through her armor. She was starting to *feel*.

To distract herself from *feeling*, she took the luxury that being alone in his apartment gave her. Brushed-metal frames adorned photos of beautiful women – four of them to be exact. One obviously was his mother. She certainly had passed the same blue eyes and dark hair to her handsome son. She was beautiful now, but Erica imaged that the woman must have been a siren in her youth. Upon closer inspection of the other three, she noticed the same family resemblance. The others must have been his sisters or cousins. Whatever the relation, there was certainly love and happiness. It was most evident in the photo of the four women with her Pretty Boy. Each one of them had their arms wrapped around his neck from different angles, and some were laughing while the others were smiling that genuine smile that she was coming to depend on. It was a perfect family moment caught by the quick lens of a camera, forever frozen. It was perfect. It was love, and that realization cut Erica to the quick.

Love. As a girl, a teenager even, she'd dreamed of it. She would find a handsome man who would love her and live to make her happy, and she would love him and make him happy in return. He would be her Prince Charming. They would marry in a big church with her in a gown worthy of her fairytale, and they would live happily ever after.

She thought she'd found love with Kurt, her high school

sweetheart. Together they were high school royalty. They were both from wealthy, influential families. They were both beautiful. He was quarterback of the football team, and she was the head cheerleader. Life was perfect, and they were perfect – until the night of the championship game.

Of course, they'd won the game. Kurt had led the team through an undefeated season. She had been sure that he was going to propose to her that night. They would marry, and he would go to college while she would be the perfect socialite wife. She had pictured everything on the way to meet Kurt at the football field that night. It was going to be the perfect place for their proposal, and years down the line, people would ooh and ah over the perfect life of the quarterback and head cheerleader..

When she'd gotten there, Kurt had been drunk. She'd never seen him like that before. To her knowledge, Kurt didn't drink. She had been so very wrong, and knew it instantly when he'd kissed her. They'd never had sex; she was saving herself for the perfect honeymoon. Oh, they'd played some, but it had never gone too far, until that night.

The beer on Kurt's breath had made her sick to her stomach,

but even worse was the way he'd groped her. He had been so rough, tearing at her clothes and flesh. She'd tried to push him away, but her size was all wrong. She was too small to push him away, and he was too strong to let her.

Erica had been raped that night by her Prince Charming in the middle of the high school football field while he slurred promises over and over again to love her forever and make her his bride. She knew that the love she had inside her disappeared that night along with her virginity. From that moment on, she swore that she would never love and would never be alone with another man unless she knew without a doubt that something like that would never happen again. There was safety in numbers.

The sound of the water turning off brought Erica back to the present and the genuine love pouring out of the picture she held in her hands. In an instant, she shook off the memory she'd forbidden herself to recall until then and climbed out of the rabbit hole before descending further down. She set the photo down carefully so as not to break the happiness spell and wandered down the hall until she found what appeared to be Robert's bedroom.

His bedroom was luxury personified. The king bed that filled the room was adorned with plush bedding and pillows. The same theme of muted colors and light wood floors spilled over into this room. Everything was beautifully done and well thought out. Robert was obviously a man of good taste, present company included.

Erica stretched out on his bed, hoping to catch his smell, but all she smelled was laundry detergent. He obviously hadn't been sleeping in his bed. A man that smelled as wonderfully masculine as he did would leave his fragrance behind. She thought back to the broken look on his sculpted face when she'd asked about overnight guests on the couch and the realization hit her: The last time he'd slept in his bed had been with a woman; one who had obviously meant something deeply to him.

"Damn, Pretty Boy," Erica muttered to herself. "You're as broken as I am; aren't you?"

Robert opened the door to the bathroom to catch the last part of Erica's musing.

"Absolutely," he answered her rhetorical question.

Erica was speechless. Robert stood in the doorway wrapped in a thick, white towel, his body glistening with the heat and humidity billowing around him in an effort to escape the confines of the bathroom. His black hair was wet and fell in curls all around his head, and she was overcome with the need to feel him.

Robert stood in the doorway looking at his own personal witch draped across his bed. Could she work her magic and expel his ghost?

Erica saw Robert start to wander away down the same trail he'd taken in the living room and was determined to bring him back to the here-and-now, so she did the only thing she knew how to do and rose up to her knees. She slowly pulled her green dress up over her head and discarded it to the floor.

Kneeling there in the middle of his bed was a vision! Erica was on her knees wearing lace green panties and a matching bra. With her green heels on her tiny feet behind her, she looked like an Irish idol given to him in a blessing, and he wanted her. Though, more than wanting her in this moment, Robert *needed* Erica. He needed her to erase the vision of Amelia from his sheets. He needed her to banish her ghost forever, and if she could be successful – *how he hoped she would be successful* – he was determined now more than ever to make Erica his.

In answer to his silent need, Erica curled her finger and cooed, "Come on, Pretty Boy. Let's have some fun and exorcise a ghost."

CHAPTER 14

Robert lay there, tied to the head of his four-poster bed with the neckties Erica had retrieved from his closet.

"Let's see what kind of music you like to listen to, Pretty Boy," Erica teased as she browsed through the music on Robert's phone he had discarded on the nightstand beside his bed on his way to the shower. Erica sorted through music from The Rolling Stones, The Eagles and CCR, smiling at further proof of Robert's good tastes, before settling on the perfect song, recalling one of the names Robert called her.

Robert smiled and settled into his pillow as the words to "Witchy Woman" floated through the room. There was no more fitting song for his captor than this.

He watched as Erica swayed to the rhythm and began her

exorcism. He could do nothing but lie there in his bed that was haunted by one woman while watching the other one dance around him. Her hands roamed her body, instruments casting her spell. The more her hands roamed, the deeper he fell. Erica glided around his bed, her green lingerie and unruly red hair such a contrast to the pale colors of his room. Seeing her there, he could finally see what his life had been missing. Her vibrancy permeated his space and filled the emptiness he had once hoped Amelia would fill.

Erica danced, and it was beautiful. She twirled around and around expertly in green heels while stroking her skin. Robert so desperately wanted to touch her, to replace her hands with his, but he was at her mercy. He knew that from the moment he'd laid eyes on her, but never was it more obvious than lying here, tied expertly at the wrists by her nimble little fingers to his unyielding headboard.

Erica spun to the foot of Robert's bed, and her entire presence changed. She transformed from playful to seductive in an instant as she kicked off her heels and crawled catlike up the bed. Robert was spellbound. This was Erica in control. She was in her element.

Erica stood up in the center of his bed, the only time she would ever tower over him, and began slowly removing her bra. Again,

Robert was caught in her spell and could not look away.

"Now, Pretty Boy, we begin. Here are the rules. One of them is akin to the one you gave me last night," Erica's voice spoke over the music surrounding them as she tossed her bra to the floor. Her breasts were glorious and out of Robert's reach, nearly distracting him from her voice.

Erica slowly began removing her lace green panties. "Are you listening?" her voice brought Robert back to her rules. "Nod if you understand."

Robert nodded.

"Good. Now, the rules," Erica began to explain. "You will not speak unless I ask you a question. To speak means that you are thinking, and the only thing I want you to do is feel. Do you understand? You may answer me."

Robert swallowed. This was the sexiest thing anyone had ever done to him, but it was also the scariest. All he knew was that he couldn't turn away. "Yes, I understand."

"One more rule, and then we can get started," Erica leveled her stare to meet Robert's. "At no time will you close your eyes. Regardless of what I am doing, you will keep them open. Regardless of what you are feeling, you will keep them open. Even if my eyes are closed, even if I cannot see you, you will keep your eyes open. Do you understand? You may answer me."

"Yes, I understand," Robert answered and settled back to let his witch work her magic.

"Now, I'm going to do what I wanted to do last night when you denied me."

Robert thought back. He could never deny her anything. What could she mean?

Erica knelt down from her height above him, and Robert watched. He kept his eyes glued to the temptress and her beautiful body while trying to anticipate her next move, and then it was apparent. Robert's heart leapt in his chest as he felt Erica's smooth nakedness slide down his legs, and he felt the weight of her breasts press down on him. He was vaguely aware of the song change as the most perfect pair of lips found the head of his cock. As relief washed over him, he was suddenly aware of the ache that had been growing while his attention was completely captivated by Erica.

He obeyed. He kept silent while watching her take him completely into her mouth. He felt her throat open to him as he hit deeply. As she swallowed him over and over, groaning her appreciation, his hands ached to grab her hair by the fistfuls. He pulled at his restraints on instinct, and the pinch reminding him of his captivity was almost as delicious as the feeling of Erica's tongue and lips as they pleasured him. Each stroke from her mouth was accentuated as she moved her body against his legs. She rolled her body with each swallow, and he felt her breasts swing into his balls. The sensation was overwhelming and spread through his entire body. Robert felt his thighs tighten with the familiar pull of his impending orgasm, and suddenly Erica stopped.

He wanted to cry out, but he remembered that he couldn't speak, lest disobey. He couldn't disobey and turn back now.

"We can't have you coming just yet. There's still work to be done," Erica punctuated her statement with a soft kiss to his lower head and sat up, straddling his thighs.

The witch took him into her hands and pressed it against her belly. Her skin was soft and hot, burning so deliciously. She rose and fell with him still pressed up against her soft flesh. She was torturing him and pleasuring him all at once. Robert wanted to close his eyes and savor the intriguing feeling, but, again, he couldn't. Instead, he distracted himself by studying Erica.

She was stunning. Lost in absolute seduction, she was expertly weaving a spell. Her body moved so smoothly, and her eyes locked to his.

"Do you like this?" she asked.

Robert nodded.

"Well, then, I know you'll love this," Erica's next fall was to slide his full length inside of her.

Robert's eyes went wide, and his mouth opened.

"Uh-uh. Remember, no speaking," she cautioned.

Robert was going to go mad. The feeling of being taken by Erica overwhelmed every one of his senses. Each time she rose up to nearly let him slip out was terrifying. He couldn't be separated from this feeling. In contrast, each time she slid slowly back down his length was like basking in the sun after a long winter. She heated him from the inside out and filled him with her fire.

Erica sped up, chasing her orgasm, and Robert wanted to follow, but he couldn't. He couldn't take his eyes off Erica. As he watched, something miraculous filled him. It was Erica's fire, and then he realized what he'd known from the instant he felt her eyes on him.

She had burned away everything that Amelia had damaged, cauterizing the gaping wound left by her rejection. Where Amelia was warm, Erica was true fire, and her fire burned so intensely.

Erica's orgasm ripped through her from the place her body met Robert's, and he felt every spasm. And just like that, Amelia's ghost was exorcised. Robert watched as the memories of Amelia's chocolate eyes and hair melted away in the heat from Erica's fire. Red, hot flames licked away everything that was Amelia, and Robert was left with unruly red hair matted in sweat to the creamiest skin he had ever seen. Erica's cries of pleasure sang to him as light once again touched the dark places in his soul, healing his wounds.

"Come on, Baby," Erica cooed as she moved through the end of her orgasm. "Give yourself over. It's your turn."

Robert surrendered completely to Erica as she rode him. Total joy filled his body as he watched her play with her breasts, enjoying her control. Her head fell back, her hair grazing the tops of his thighs, and as she arched her back, Robert surrendered to himself. The orgasm that took control of him was more powerful than anything he'd ever felt. The emotion that accompanied the orgasm overwhelmed him and brought tears to his eyes.

He was crying.

Dammit.

Erica collapsed on top of Robert and relished the last pulse of his pleasure. She just thought that this little experiment would be fun, a great way to spend a Saturday afternoon while introducing Robert to a little of Mistress Erica. She was completely unprepared for the emotion that washed over her when she saw the tears stream from his eyes.

With him still inside of her, she dared a look up into Robert's face and was taken aback with what she saw. There was that smile that she was growing to absolutely adore ripping his beautiful face in two, reaching into his moist eyes. But what was even more powerful was the emotion radiating from him. It was the same emotion she had seen in the photos from before. It was the same emotion she had fantasized about as a child. Even more powerful still was the emotion she felt in return.

Love.

Shit!

CHAPTER 15

Robert held the most precious woman in his arms and listened to the music serenade them. The song choice was, again, perfect for how he felt in this moment. The Black Crows sang about a miracle, and he knew exactly what they meant because he was holding one. In less than twenty-four short hours, Erica had not only cured his heartache, but she had also filled his heart. Surely, he couldn't be the only one feeling it.

"You're awfully quiet," Robert broke the silence.

"Mmmm," was Erica's only reply.

Robert could tell that she was deep in thought. What he wouldn't give to know what she was mulling over; yet, all he knew was that she was too distant. He needed her thoughts to be as close to him as her body was.

"Hey," he tried to reach her again. "Earth to Erica."

His voice brought her back from her mental journey.

"Sorry," Erica muttered.

"It's okay," Robert pulled her tighter. "Where were you?"

"Who was she?" Erica blurted out.

Well, that wasn't what he was expecting. Robert tensed for a moment while wondering whether he should open up about Amelia and then relaxed with his decision.

"I take it back. You don't have to tell me about her," Erica offered quickly, suddenly afraid of the answer.

"No, it's okay," Robert began as the song changed again. "I want to. I mean, after all, why should I hide anything from you now? I feel like you've seen my soul, and you're still here."

Erica sat up, and Robert joined her. There they sat naked in the middle of his bed huddled like girls at a slumber party getting ready to share the latest gossip. Though for them, it was much more powerful.

Robert began.

"It was doomed from the start. She was married, and I was competing with over five years of history."

Erica muttered, "Been there."

Amusement softened Robert's face. "Really?"

"Really," Erica laughed. "On both sides."

Robert looked puzzled.

"Both the husband *and* the wife," Erica clarified.

The thought of Erica with another woman threatened to redirect his blood flow, and his penis twitched.

"Nah-uh," Erica chastised. "First spill it, and then we'll see about him."

"Fair enough," Robert chuckled and then steeled himself for the rest of the story. "She was a co-worker, too."

"Ouch," Erica interjected. "Double-whammy."

"Are you going to let me tell the story, or am I going to have to tie you down and gag you?" he only half-teased. He certainly wanted to return the bondage favor.

"Sorry. I'll be quiet, but we'll revisit that scenario later," Erica winked.

Robert realized that he needed to tell the story to someone. He needed to speak the words and release them. That freedom, combined with Erica's healing, would be his redemption.

"I fell for her before I even knew what had happened. Her

husband put her on the back burner to his career, and I just wanted to take away her pain. One night, he rejected her for what I thought would be the final time, and she came to me. Here. We spent a couple of hours rolling around in bed, and then she left.

I didn't hear from her for two days, and then that Monday at work, she gave me the it-never-should-have-happened speech. It was like the whole thing happened in slow motion and in fast-forward all at the same time. I said some pretty shitty stuff, and that was it. Amelia transferred offices the same day, and I haven't seen her since, except in my dreams, but you cured that," Robert said all in one breath.

Erica sat listening intently to the story until the name 'Amelia' hit her.

"Wait a minute. Wait a minute," Erica began, and Robert froze. "Amelia? What did she look like?" *Surely she couldn't be* THAT *Amelia.*

Robert proceeded with caution. He knew nothing about Erica. Surely she wasn't Amelia's long-lost sister or something. Even though alarms were going off in his head, he answered Erica's question.

"Long brown hair, big brown eyes," he began.

"Kissable lips, curvy in all the right places, husband named John," Erica finished.

Robert leaned back to put some distance between them. "How?"

"Dammit! Well, it's no wonder why you had trouble getting her out of your system. She was one great fuck," Erica said with surprise.

Robert looked at her in disbelief and bewilderment. "You? And Amelia? And *John*?" John was said with the hatred Robert felt for the man. Surely the bastard couldn't have had Amelia *and* Erica. The world wasn't that small, and he wasn't going to compete for another woman's heart in John Foster's wake.

Erica waved her hands to bring Robert back from the dark place he was going. "Amelia and me, yes. John got to watch and touch a little. There was no," and she scooted across the bed to close the gap between her and Robert, "this," she finished.

Relief flooded over Robert's face and softened his posture. "Oh, thank God!" he exclaimed and crushed Erica to him while he tried to calculate the odds of the two women who had affected him more than anything having been lovers. Deciding they were too astronomical, he asked, "How? When?"

Erica took a breath before answering. Amelia had hurt Robert deeply, and she suddenly hated the woman for having power over John *and* Robert. Who the hell was she to tell John what he could and could not do while hurting Robert so deeply, leaving him to his pain like some sort of collateral damage?! But, looking at Robert now, all she saw was curiosity. The pain that haunted him hours before was gone, and that gave her the strength to control her anger.

"A little over a month or so ago, I guess. It was the same scenario as you and Ginger. I picked them up at the club one Saturday night and invited them back to my place. I usually don't do married couples because it gets complicated, but there was something about them. We played around for an evening, and then I sent them home." It was Erica's turn to spill everything in one breath.

Robert sat there and let it all sink in. *Wow.* "So, did you hear about her accident?"

"Yes. They were actually leaving my house when it happened," she answered and then wished she could have taken it back.

"Your *house*? You mean your *apartment*? But the accident didn't happen anywhere near the city. It was in the middle of nowhere."

Erica swallowed and prayed for a distraction – any distraction. Her nakedness wasn't working here because they were having the entire conversation naked, and then her stomach answered her prayer with a growl. "Can we talk about that *after* some food? I'm starving. We worked breakfast off."

Robert laughed at the tiny woman with the large appetite. "Sure, but we're not as lucky here," Robert frowned. "My kitchen is not as stocked as yours. I'm afraid we'll have to go out for dinner."

"Well, what are we waiting for?" Erica jumped up at the same time one of Robert's favorite songs began to play.

"Let's go," he jumped out of bed, scooped Erica up into his arms and bent to whisper in her ear, "But first, we dance."

Robert pulled Erica's naked body close to his and swayed back and forth, singing softly along with John Fogerty as he sang,

First time that I saw you, ooh, you took my breath away.

I might not get to heaven, but I walked with the angels that day.

She takes me by the hand; I am the luckiest man alive.

And did I tell you baby, you are the joy of my life.

Erica was lost in Robert's soft voice in her ear singing the most beautiful words, the feel of her body pressed against his and the overwhelming warmth filling her from the inside out. Suddenly, the emptiness in her stomach was replaced by the longing she felt for the man in her arms, and she pulled him back to his bed.

Dinner could wait.

CHAPTER 16

"Wake up, Sleeping Beauty," Robert placed a hot cup of coffee on the nightstand, sat on Erica's side of his bed and whispered in her ear.

He was rewarded with a sexy, "Mmmm…," although he knew it was for the smell of the coffee and not for him. *Well*, he thought, *not ALL for the coffee*, and smiled.

What a difference a few days had made. He'd spent Thursday night drunk on a barstool pouring salt into the wounds Amelia had left, and on Sunday morning he was waking the most amazing woman he'd ever met from sleeping in his bed. Though all he wanted to do was crawl back in bed next to her, he was too excited about what the day would bring, and he wanted to bring it in with Erica. After what she'd done for him last night, banishing Amelia's ghost from his bed, his dreams and his heart, he couldn't wait to start the fresh, new day. It was going to be a day without heartache, a day to be spent surrounded by laughter and love, and he couldn't think of anyone he'd rather spend it with than his Sleeping Beauty. But first, she had to wake up.

"If you don't open those beautiful blue eyes of yours, I'm going to resort to corny, fairytale tactics, Princess" he mockingly threatened.

A grin tugged at Erica's lips. "I thought you'd never get the hint, Pretty Boy. I mean, really, where were you when they were handing out brains…"

Robert cut her off with a sweet, good-morning kiss that quickly deepened into something more. His body began responding to her beckoning tongue as if it were a finger curling in a tantalizing invitation. Unfortunately for him, this morning, he had been present when they were handing out brains, and his brain happened to be winning the battle. It truly was a Sunday miracle! He had somewhere to be today, and he was taking Erica with him.

Reluctantly breaking the kiss before Erica could turn the tide, Robert put the coffee cup under her nose and watched her come to life.

Erica put the cup to her lips and closed her eyes as she took her first sip. He'd gotten it just right – sweet and creamy. Opening her eyes and seeing him looking at her with such excitement, she was once again taken by just how handsome he was. His blue eyes were extra bright this morning, but she attributed that to the fact that they never made it to dinner last night after his sweet serenade. She would have never guessed that it was –

"I want you to meet my family," Robert blurted out.

Erica spat her coffee back into her cup and searched his eyes for the punch line. There was none. There was only excitement, tempered with a little nervousness, if she had to guess.

Robert continued without giving her a chance to interrupt. "I always spend Sunday with my family -- my mom and my sisters, to be precise. We have an early dinner, some delicious dessert and then spend some time just visiting. It's a beautiful day. I want you to go with me."

Again, Erica waited for the punch line. If she knew anything about herself, it was that she was not the take-home-to-your-mother type. She was the mistress, the secret-kept-from-a-doting-wife type for sure, but not this.

"Robert…" she began, and he cut her off by removing the cup from her hands and setting it back down on its spot on the nightstand.

Robert wanted Erica to spend the day with him so badly that he ached. To see her in the little home he'd grown up in, surrounded by the four women who saw him through his best and his worst with unwavering love and support would mean everything to him. So, he tried the one thing that made her give in to him before, on their first night together, the one that seemed so long ago.

"Erica, please," Robert begged without shame. "I spend every Sunday with my mom and my sisters. They are the most important people in my life, and I want you to meet them. I want *them* to meet *you.* " He closed his eyes and opened them slowly to punctuate his longing for her to say yes before adding, "Please, Erica."

Dammit! Erica had always had a filthy mouth, but since she'd met Robert Friday night, she'd cussed much more than usual – noticeably at herself for giving in to him when she knew better. She should have just left the club without casting a second glance at him, and then she wouldn't be sitting here …

… Staring into the deepest blue eyes that reflected the soul of the man who sent her flying through the air on his shoulders, put her desires first, sang to her the sweetest song and, most important, looked at her like she was *more*.

"How can I say no when you beg like that?" Erica teased, and the nervousness left Robert's eyes.

He carefully crushed her to him, and Erica could feel relief flood through his muscles as she held him momentarily before the excitement, once again, dominated.

"There's a clean T-shirt at the foot of the bed for you. I made breakfast out of what I could find; I hope you like cheese toast. I'll have to go shopping for food. You can grab a shower while I clean up after breakfast," Robert was speeding through so quickly that Erica was losing track.

"Whoa, there, Pretty Boy. A shower? I need to go back to my place and grab some clean clothes and freshen up if I'm going to meet your mother," Erica reminded him while inwardly shrieking at the foreign words coming from her mouth.

"Oh, there's no time for that. While you were sleeping, I washed your clothes from last night and ran down to the gas station at the corner and grabbed you a toothbrush and some deodorant," Robert said as he walked to the dresser and picked up the saucers containing their breakfast. "Now, eat up before it gets cold, and we can get going."

Erica was flabbergasted. "Toothbrush? Deodorant? What the hell? What time is it?" She looked around for some sign of the day, but Robert had pulled the drapes closed sometime during the night.

"It's noon. I let you sleep as long as I could," he brushed her hair back from her shoulders. "You were so beautiful that I hated to wake you, but we really need to go. I already called and told Mom to set an extra place at the table this afternoon."

Erica was trying to keep up. With only a couple of sips of coffee, it was proving to be a Herculean task. *Phone? Phone! Where was her phone?* She'd never gone that long without getting a thousand texts, at least...most of them from Brock. She looked around frantically. It had to be there somewhere!

"What are you looking for?" Robert was puzzled by her frenzy. "You've got food, coffee and clean laundry. What more could you want?"

Erica stopped and looked at Robert. He really was pretty, but she had to find her phone. "My phone. It's got to be around here somewhere."

Relief once again softened Robert's posture.

"It's probably in the living room. You set your purse on the couch when we got here yesterday. It's probably still in there. Wait here. I'll go get it."

Robert disappeared down the hall and sprinted back a moment later with her purse, which, much to Erica's relief, contained her phone. She pulled it out and inspected the damage.

"Could I have a moment alone to return some messages?" she asked Robert.

He nodded, grabbed his share of breakfast and left the room.

There were 53 texts, and at least 50 of them were from Brock. The last one was from fifteen minutes ago threatening to send out a search party if she didn't respond. Oh, she had to stop that. Brock's worry meeting with Robert's possession would not end well.

She typed out a quick response and then followed it with a longer one.

I'M OK.

CALL OFF THE SEARCH PARTY. I'LL FILL YOU IN LATER. :)

The response was almost immediate.

THANK GOD!

Immediately followed by a playful threat.

YOU'LL DESERVE THE NEXT SPANKING. ;)

Erica's sigh was filled with the relief that washed over her. Brock was taken care of for the moment, and he seemed to be appeased. The other texts were from the guards at the club – her club. She shot off answers to them and let them know that she was, indeed, okay. They always kept a watchful eye and checked on her when they knew she left with new people, and they were sounding quite concerned. What wonderful brutes! She'd have to sweeten their paychecks.

With her world assured of her physical safety, she was growing a more concerned about her sanity as she finished her bites of cheese toast and walked toward Robert's bathroom to prepare to meet his family – his *mother*.

She darted back to the bed and picked up her phone to make a quick call and rolled her eyes when she got voicemail. Everyone really should be available when she needed them, she thought while waiting as patiently as she could for the beep.

"Dr. Boyd, this is Erica. Erica Spencer. Call me when you get this. Something's happened, and I'm afraid that I won't be able to wait until Friday for our next appointment. I need to see you as soon as possible." Erica paused for a moment and then said something that was not usually a part of her vocabulary, "Please."

Erica hit the END button, tossed the phone on the bed, where she desperately longed to remain, and headed to the shower feeling her sanity slowly slipping…

… Or was it her heart?

Maybe they were one in the same, she thought as she turned the shower on and let the hot water wash her musings down the drain.

CHAPTER 17

Erica stood in the small living room that comfortably accompanied space in the tiny house where Robert had spent his childhood. Family photos smiled back at her. Knick-knacks whispered of trips taken and fun had. Everything about the house told her that this was a home, and a happy one at that.

After scanning the room's memories, one photo beckoned Erica's attention. It was of Robert's mother, Sylvia, in the quintessential, big wedding gown holding onto the arm of who could have only been Robert's father. Robert was the perfect mix of his parents. He had his mother's blue eyes and dark hair, but everything else was his father's, from the tall frame and broad shoulders to the genuine, heart-stopping smile that Erica had quickly come to love. Other than the few times Robert had gifted her with that smile since Friday night, the one on his father's face as the camera caught him stealing a glimpse of his beaming bride was the most genuine Erica had ever seen. The love in the picture nearly broke Erica's heart.

"He was a handsome one, my Robert," a nostalgic voice tore Erica away from the photo.

She turned and was face-to-face with Robert's mother. Sylvia was a beautiful woman in her early sixties who had aged quite well. Her eyes were still brilliantly blue, and a thick mane of black hair lightly dusted with gray framed her pretty face. She smiled at Erica to help her feel comfortable, but Erica could see the longing behind the warm smile.

"Robert was named after his father?" Erica asked.

"Both your Robert and my Robert were named after their fathers," Sylvia answered, her eyes never leaving the photo. "Robert Alexander Cunningham. Such a strong name. It was important to my husband that his son carried his name, and with a smile like that … oh, I just couldn't deny him anything, but I'm sure you understand. My son does have his father's smile." Nostalgia once again deepened her words.

Erica smiled back and nodded. She completely understood. She'd done many things over the past few days that were out of character for her because of that smile. Standing here took the cake.

"Robert hasn't said anything, so may I ask --" Erica began.

"About his father? Of course, but let's sit, please, if you don't mind," his mother answered.

Erica glanced uneasily toward the kitchen. She'd certainly never been left alone with someone's mother before.

"Oh, don't worry about them. Robert and his sisters are wonderful in the kitchen. They make me dinner every Sunday, and it will be done before you know it," Sylvia said over the chorus of sibling laughter coming from the kitchen.

Erica followed Sylvia to the couch and sat down beside her on the offered cushion. Sadness washed over the woman's beautiful features before she closed her eyes and took a deep breath. When she opened them, the sadness was gone, replaced by the comfort of the upcoming love story.

"Robert's father and I were the product of a whirlwind romance. We met when he came to town to visit some friends, and his friends knew my friends. There was a party, our eyes met across the room, and that was it. I was his from that moment forward."

Erica fidgeted in her seat at the familiarity of the story. Yet, instead of a party, it was a club, but as soon as Erica had laid eyes on Robert, she'd wanted him.

Sylvia smiled knowingly and continued her story.

"Our families were not 100% thrilled that we wanted to get married after such a short courtship, but why waste time? When you know it's right, no amount of time will change that; right? With such a limited amount of time together, I'm so glad that we didn't listen to them," the sadness made its return, but the storyteller shook it off and smiled. "But, I'm getting ahead of myself; aren't I?"

Such sadness mixed with such happiness. Erica reminded herself why she closed off her heart after the night Kurt broke her. She didn't want sadness to ever contaminate her happiness. But looking back now, after seeing honest-to-God happiness caught in a candid wedding photo, had she ever truly been happy?

"We bought this house right after our honeymoon and couldn't wait to start our family," Sylvia continued. "My Robert actually made the rocking chairs on the front porch because he said that wanted to sit there in the evenings and watch our kids play and grow old with me and watch our grandkids play. He would say, 'I'll bet you'll be even more beautiful with every gray hair put there by me and our kids.' Of course, we didn't have kids yet, but he could just see them; ya know?"

Erica just smiled. She didn't know. She had grown up an only child, and her parents divorced before she was out of elementary school. Since then, both of her parents had had several partners. Family was *not* an aspiration of Erica's.

"Well, not long after the rocking chairs came Sandy. The twins, Elizabeth and Frances, came just a year later. Robert loved his girls, and they had him wrapped around their little fingers, but I knew he wanted a son to carry on his name. So, we tried for one more, and the next year, Robert was born. Now, you can imagine with four children nipping on each other's heels, I had my hands full. Robert worked at the mill, and I stayed home with the kids. Oh, I painted some on the side and even sold some here or there, usually around Christmas to earn some extra money to help Santa out," the older lady winked, and Erica smiled to rid herself of the sinking feeling growing in her stomach at the mention of the mill. Growing up, she'd heard of a terrible explosion. Sylvia picked up on Erica's unease and nodded.

"Sandy was 8, making my little man only 6 years old. We could actually feel the explosion from the gas main when it happened. It woke the kids from their naps, and I had a devil of a time getting them back to sleep that afternoon. Then, once they were good and asleep, the knock at the door woke them up again. I was so frustrated, but everything stopped when I saw Robert's boss standing there with his hat in his hands. Apparently, Robert and some coworkers had been having lunch outside when the gas main nearby exploded. He and everyone around him were killed instantly. The mill was shut down for an investigation, and he was so very sorry for my loss."

Tears threatened the brilliant blue eyes staring at the photo on the mantle, but she continued. "Anyway, that was it. There was a good pension, and the other wives and I got a generous settlement from the city and the mill. That allowed me to stay home with my babies and paid for their educations. Every one of them has a college education," Sylvia said with pride and looked around the room at her memories.

Erica let her have her moment and felt her fondness for this woman grow exponentially. Now, that was hardship. That was pain. But, it was also triumph and pride. She obviously loved her family so much that she kept going because of them, but one question nagged Erica. Her curiosity got the best of her, and she had to ask it.

"So, you never remarried?" Erica asked.

Sylvia turned to look at Erica and grabbed Erica's shoulders to punctuate whatever she was about to say.

"Sweetheart, once you've had once-in-a-lifetime love, nothing else can compare. Yes, our time together was cut short, but it was wonderful, and I wouldn't trade it for anything. I see him and our love in our children every single day. That's immortality. That's how you live forever … not through Botox or anything money can buy, but through love. Oh, I've been on a date or three; I'm no spinster, but no one will ever compare to my Robert."

Erica let Sylvia's words sink in. Once-in-a-lifetime love was only in fairytales, in the books she read as a girl, the ones with dragons and castles and shining knights. But sitting here, Erica could feel that once-in-a-lifetime love surrounding her from every part of the small home, and it still radiated, all these years later, from the heart of this woman who loved – and was loved by – her husband so deeply. Erica wasn't sure whether this made her happy to know that it truly existed or sad because she knew that she wasn't meant for that kind of love. All she knew was that she felt its presence.

Still holding Erica, Sylvia said, "What does a mother's heart good is that I've seen that look again today."

Erica was baffled. *What? When? Who?*

Sylvia turned Erica to look at Robert, who was leaning in the doorway that separated the kitchen and the living room, surrounded by his sisters' curious eyes. There was that smile. Erica could definitely see his father's smile, but what was even more distracting was the fact that she could also see the same love shining from his eyes that she just witnessed in his mother's. He truly was the perfect blend of his parents.

Sylvia broke Erica's inspection before she could dig deeper into the implications. "Smells delicious! Come on, Sweetheart. Let's wash up. It seems dinner is served." She rubbed her hands together and headed toward the kitchen, stopping to kiss her son on his cheek along the way.

A true gentleman, Robert dipped his head so that his mother would not have to tiptoe to reach his cheek and then allowed her room to pass.

He held out his hand to Erica.

"Shall we?"

Erica looked at his outstretched hand and pondered the question for a moment. It seemed much heavier than it should have been. But, before she could delve any further, her stomach growled. Her last full meal had been pancakes Saturday morning, and the smell of fried chicken and homemade biscuits roused her appetite.

Robert laughed.

"I'll take that as a yes," he jested and pulled Erica to her feet and into his arms in one move.

Erica was breathless for a moment.

"I love your mom," she said, and the sentiment surprised her.

Robert's face broke into a proud grin.

"Me, too. She's pretty fantastic; isn't she?"

There was no pretense or attitude in his response. It was simply the genuine love of a son for his mother combined with pride. Erica's heart swelled.

"Let's eat, Princess," Robert whispered in her ear. He filled it with such carnality that Erica blushed at the thought.

"What? Are you blushing? After everything we've done? Really?" Robert teased.

Erica's blush deepened.

"We're standing in your mother's living room," she said in a whisper. "You can't do that!"

"Then I *really* shouldn't do this," Robert laughed and bent to kiss Erica.

It was slow and sweet and melted her knees as if they were the butter on the biscuits that were just taken out of the oven.

"You definitely can't do that!" she slapped him in the middle of his chest.

"Noted," Robert smiled. "Now, let's eat. I don't know about you, but I am absolutely starving!"

On cue, his mother appeared in the doorway.

"Come on, you two. There's plenty of time to do that later," she winked as sadness ran across her face. After hearing her love story, Erica felt the gravity in Sylvia's words, knowing that there was never enough time when you truly loved someone – *not that she loved someone*, she was sure to correct herself.

It was her turn to grab Robert's hand and pull him toward the kitchen.

"Let's go, Pretty Boy. Feed me!"

CHAPTER 18

Robert sat in one of the rockers on the front porch of his childhood home listening to his mother and his sisters engage Erica in light conversation. Erica was comfortably holding her own with his most favorite women in the world. A light autumn breeze was blowing, and everyone was enjoying dessert after a delicious dinner. The sun was just starting to set, casting a warm, orange hue across a cloud-filled sky.

Of course, he'd received the third degree from Sandy, Elizabeth and Frances while they were cooking.

"Tell me that she's not the one who turned you into a zombie the last few months," Sandy had said, and Robert had been quick to assure her that it was quite the opposite. Erica had been the one to bring him back to life. All three of his sisters had feigned swooning with his assurance, and their usual teasing and laughter resumed. He loved his sisters so very much. Growing up with them and being raised by a single mother showed him how very valuable and precious women are. Growing up without a father and hearing his parents' love story showed him how short and precious life truly was. He liked to think that both made him a good man and would make him a good husband and father someday.

Erica ate the last bite of her chocolate cake and caramel-covered vanilla ice cream thinking back to her musings yesterday morning – *Had it really been only yesterday?!* – as she laid curled up to Robert after their first night together thinking that she liked feeling him more than a second-helping of ooey-gooey dessert while sitting in a rocking chair on the porch during an autumn Sunday afternoon and nearly choked trying to hold in her laughter. She never imagined that she would actually BE sitting in a rocking chair on someone's front porch on an autumn Sunday afternoon eating a bowl of ooey-gooey dessert! She might even have to ask for a second helping just to see if she was right. However, feeling the tightening of her stomach thinking about lying naked next to Robert assured her that she would still like him more, no matter how absolutely delicious the homemade chocolate cake had been.

As if on cue, Sylvia asked Erica if she would like more cake and ice cream.

"Oh, no thank you, truly," Erica said politely. "I'm absolutely stuffed!"

"Besides," Robert said in Erica's defense before his mother could protest, "we really need to get going. It looks like a storm is trying to roll in, and, besides, it's the girls' turn to wash dishes. I need to get Erica home."

Robert rose to take Erica's dishes and disappeared into the house.

"You really must come again," Sylvia said and rose to kiss Erica's cheek. "I've just enjoyed your company so much, and it's been wonderful to see my boy so happy."

Robert came back out the front door in time to catch the last part of his mother's comment.

"Mom, please don't scare her off," he said and winked at Erica before adding, "I really like this one."

His sisters joined in a chorus of teasing as he kissed each one on the cheek and bent to envelop his mother in a loving embrace.

Erica marveled at the comfortable affection shared between each of them. Her family was so the opposite. Her father, though he loved her dearly, was not an affectionate man, and her mother would rather just send her expensive gifts from overseas than fly home for a visit or hug her daughter. With no siblings or close cousins, family love was a no-contact sport for Erica. Seeing Robert and his family, though, made her long – if only for a moment – for something she'd never had. As if sensing the change in her mood, a chilly rain started to fall from the darkening clouds above.

Robert pulled himself from his mother's arms and grabbed Erica's hand. Warmth instantly ran from his touch up her arm making the rain seem less chilly. The heat from Robert's innocent touch began to spread through her body, keeping her warm as they sprinted through the increasing downpour to his car.

"Buckle up, Princess," Robert said to her as he slid into the driver's seat and shut the door. "The sky looks like it's getting ready to split wide open, and I'd love to get you home and out of those wet clothes before it does."

Erica loved the fact that he could make such a simple, caring statement sound so filthy. She loved how he looked drenched with rain even more.

"I think it's the 'out of those wet clothes' part that you're actually looking forward to," Erica teased as the Camaro's engine announced their departure with a throaty roar.

Robert slipped the car effortlessly into first gear and eased around his mother's circular driveway. "Well, can you blame me?" a grin pulled at the corners of his beautiful mouth.

"Well, not really. I've had me, and I'm *really* good," Erica shrugged her shoulders.

The laughter ripped through Robert, forcing his playful grin into a full-blown, face-splitting smile. "Yes. Yes, you have, and I've witnessed it," he said, referencing the sight that greeted him when he opened the door to an unsuspecting Erica as she was pleasing herself. "And, just for the record, 'good' is the understatement of the century, in my humble opinion."

"Why, thank you, Pretty Boy. You're not so bad yourself."

Erica turned on the radio and ended the playful teasing while Robert carefully navigated the wet country roads. The rain continued to pelt the car as the sun finally dipped behind the horizon.

"I can't see a damned thing," Robert mumbled to himself, barely audible over the music from the radio. Had Erica not been studying his profile in the safety of the darkness, she would have missed it.

"Well, then, why don't you pull over until it eases up some, and then we'll start again? I'd really like to get home in one piece," she teased.

Robert looked over at Erica like she'd just cured world hunger, and worry eased from his forehead. "I think I will. What would I do without you?"

"Probably end up in a ditch, and that would be cruel for you, me and this beautiful machine," Erica replied.

Robert laughed again. He absolutely loved how she made him laugh. "You're probably right."

"Probably, my ass. Though, if you would've let me drive, we would have been home by now."

Robert stopped laughing and considered Erica's words. No one else had ever driven his car. He'd never even entertained the idea of allowing someone else drive his car.

"What?" Erica asked.

"No one else has ever driven my car for as long as I've had her," Robert answered truthfully. "Besides, you've been so spoiled and pampered that I can't imagine you could drive stick."

It was Erica's turn to laugh. It was fierce and hot, just like the woman from whom it erupted. Robert couldn't take his eyes off the force of nature to his right.

As her laughter died down, Erica unbuckled her seatbelt and completely turned to face Robert. "So, you don't think I can handle a *stick*?" The mood shifted in the car as thunder began to rumble in the distance.

Erica reached over and hit the button to release Robert's seatbelt. The click echoed through the car, heralding Erica's intention.

Robert's brain was quickly beginning to lose its blood supply, so, while he could still form intelligible words, he asked, "What are you doing?"

Erica leveled her stare to Robert's eyes as her fingers began to expertly unbuckle the belt at his waist.

"Drop 'em, Pretty Boy. I'll show you how I handle a stick."

CHAPTER 19

Erica's clothes rested in a pile on the passenger's floorboard as she nimbly climbed over the center console. She hadn't waited for Robert to get completely naked before climbing into his lap, her back resting against his chest. Robert's jeans and boxers were down around his ankles, but his black polo remained.

Erica gripped the Camaro's steering wheel in both hands and looked over her shoulder at a very entertained Robert. The humor in his eyes flashed brighter as lightning lit up the sky.

"Hold on, Pretty Boy. This is going to be a great ride," she winked and lowered herself to take him in.

"Thisssss…" Erica hissed as she adjusted to Robert's length, "is neutral. I usually wiggle it back and forth a little before slipping into gear." She illustrated her point beautifully by slowly rocking her hips side to side.

Robert groaned and threw his head back against the headrest. He fit so tightly into her that each rock of her hips was heaven. His big hands roamed up her tiny waist and found her heavy breasts. He squeezed each nipple hard and was rewarded with Erica's squeal.

"I guess that means you're ready to ride," she hissed again and reached down between her legs with one hand to softly massage his balls.

Robert groaned again. Between the feeling of fitting so tightly into Erica's wetness and her putting just the right amount of pressure on his testicles, he was nothing but electrical sensation from his head to his toes.

"We mustn't forget the clutch," Erica said as she stopped massaging and squeezed while simultaneously shifting her hips to the left and forward. "But every good driver knows that you never fully release the clutch between first and second gears."

She slid up and down his solid length quickly, never releasing her grip on his sack. Erica squeezed again and shifted her hips a fraction to the right and then back. She let go and placed both hands on the steering wheel for leverage. Her back rested against Robert's chest as she stroked his cock with her warm, wet insides.

Robert closed his eyes as the scent of her hair washed over him while he kneaded her breasts. Erica cried out unintelligibly. Her sensual sounds were the most beautiful sounds he'd ever heard, and he loved being the cause of them.

"Second never lasts long, either."

Erica brought him out of his worship as she reached down and grabbed him again before shifting her hips forward and leaning into the steering wheel.

Robert opened his eyes and marveled at the perfect view the position gave him. Her red hair flamed down her back, a stark contrast to her ivory skin. He released his hold on her breasts to grip her hips as she rode. Her perfectly round ass jiggled each time she took him completely in, and it took all of his restraint to maintain control. Besides, she still had two more gears to go!

"How do you handle fourth gear, Princess?" He egged her on.

She slammed back against him hard and looked at him over her shoulder.

"Like this," she reached down and grabbed him harder before shifting her hips to the right and then back against him. Both hands back on the steering wheel, she began to ride faster. "Good. God. You. Handle. So. Fucking. Great," Erica bit out between thrusts.

Robert was beyond words and completely overcome by sensation.

"Let's cruise," Erica grabbed him once more and squeezed so hard that it was Robert's turn to cry out, shifted her hips to the right and forward. "Fifth gear, Pretty Boy. Let's see what this baby can do!"

Erica picked up speed, and Robert gripped her hips hard to hold on as she sped up, moving faster and faster.

"Fuck! Robert!" Erica screamed as thunder rolled across the sky.

Robert released one of Erica's hips and found her clit with his roaming fingers. He rubbed against her, desperately needing her to come before he found his release. He squeezed the swollen pleasure nub between his thumb and forefinger.

"Dammit! Ahhhh!" Erica swore as the squeeze sent shockwaves through her entire body, announcing her impending orgasm. Robert squeezed once more, and the orgasm split from her core and shattered its way through her body. "Fuck. Fuck. Fuck. Fuck…" Erica faded into a whisper as the quake slowed to a tremor and then settled.

"Thank. God!" Robert cried as he lost his will to keep from coming. Erica's spasming walls drove him to the edge of his sanity, and he was sure he would fall off the cliff into screaming madness if he didn't climax immediately. He growled as his release came.

Erica wiggled her hips to each twitch of Robert's spilling erection before collapsing back against his chest and laid there quietly as their breathing calmed.

She went to shift and go back to her seat, but Robert trapped her in his arms.

"Not yet," he whispered in her ear before kissing it softly.

Erica shrugged and settled back against Robert. The rain was a soft drizzle now, and the thunder was just a soft rumble in the distance. It would be safe to make the drive home now, but she wasn't in any hurry for the weekend to end. She was in the arms of one of the sweetest, most gorgeous men she'd ever met who seemed to be exactly where he wanted to be. She knew that Monday would bring real life. He would return to his. She would return to hers, and nothing would ever be the same. However, just for this moment, in this car, in Robert's arms, everything was perfect.

Sensing Erica's softening, Robert kissed her ear and whispered, "You know I never want to let you go; right?"

Erica tensed a little and tried to move. Robert gripped her tighter, and she giggled.

"I'm not going to go anywhere. I just want to look at you."

Robert reluctantly let her go and winced as their intimate connection was broken. Erica maneuvered around and sat back down on his lap, this time facing him. He wasn't back inside of her, but at least he could feel her.

"You know this position is only physically possible because you're insanely tall, and I'm vertically challenged," she said to ease the deepening mood inside the car.

Robert smiled softly, but he couldn't shake the feeling that she was going to break his heart tonight. It was as if the storm that had raged through their lovemaking had found a new place inside his chest, and the clouds were starting to build.

"Erica," he began.

"Shhh, let me say something, please," Erica interrupted and put her hands on his shoulders. She needed to find a way to let him go so that she could protect both of them. Erica closed her eyes and took a deep breath for strength while searching her soul for the right words.

When she opened her eyes, what she saw nearly broke her shielded heart. The playful, carefree face that she had studied all day had been replaced with the broken face that she saw in Robert's apartment when she'd asked about an overnight guest. She had been so angry at the person who'd marred his face with such gloom, but the face in front of her tonight was her doing. A wave of tears swelled behind her eyes and broke through.

"Robert, you don't know me," she choked through her beginning tears.

He opened his mouth to speak, and she closed it with her finger.

"Let me finish, please. I am a terribly broken, terribly messed-up brat. I have so much baggage that I can't even begin to carry it all. I've buried my issues under sex and money, and I don't know anything else. I don't know how to *be* anyone else. But you -- oh my god -- you came into my life this weekend and turned everything upside down. Seeing you look at me the way you have this weekend has been wonderful. You almost make me believe that I am not so much of a mess, that I am worthy of love. *Almost*."

Erica's shoulders slumped under the weight of her confession, and years of trapped tears poured down her face. Countless therapists would have killed to have witnessed her breakthrough.

Robert crushed Erica to his chest and held her as she cried. He was trying to process her self-deprecating words and resolve them to the woman he'd spent the weekend falling in love with. He'd known all along that there was something underneath to make such a beautiful woman troll for multiple lovers and then send them away the next day, but he didn't care. It didn't matter to him what it had taken to bring them together. That was all in the past. Surely, he'd done some questionable things he wasn't so proud of, seducing a married woman and trying to lure her away from her husband being the most recent.

"Hey, don't cry," Robert rubbed her back to soothe her pain. "Look at me, please."

Erica looked up into the kindest eyes.

"Now it's my turn, and I want *you* to listen to *me*. You, Erica, are the most beautiful, intoxicating, breathtaking woman I've ever met. You make me laugh. You have a quick wit and a sharp tongue. You keep me on my toes. You surprise me. You make me surprise myself. From the moment I met you, I've wondered if you were a witch because you've had me under your spell from the first time I felt your eyes on me.

So, you're broken and a mess. How many people reach their

30s and aren't? I want my mess to be mixed up in your mess. I'll help you pick up your pieces if you help me pick up mine. Hell, I'll even help you carry your baggage, and we don't even have to unpack it. I don't need to know what you have packed away unless you want to show me. All I know is that whatever you have been through has made you who you are right now, and I happen to really, really like who I've spent the weekend with."

Erica couldn't believe the words coming out of Robert's absolutely beautiful mouth, but she wanted them to be true with all of her heart.

Her heart.

Her heart had been shielded for so many years to protect it from pain, but in one weekend, this beautiful man had broken through her defenses. Everything he had done felt right. Every word he'd spoken had seemed so truthful. Even if he had been a good enough actor to pretend when they were alone together, she'd seen him with his family. This man knew love. He knew *how* to love, and it seemed now that he wanted to give love – *to her*. Was she capable of not only accepting his love, but also of giving love in return? She'd tried that once, and it had left her a broken, dirty mess in the middle of a high school football field.

Robert watched intently as Erica warred with herself, and he wanted desperately to know what was going on inside of her head. She was so beautiful, but for the first time, he could see some of the pain behind her mask of makeup and sarcasm. She had certainly been hurt in her past, and he could see that it had been much more than a broken heart or two. He wanted to take that away from her. He wanted to make her happy. He wanted her to let him love her and to love him back. She was so passionate, fierce and awe-inspiring. Surely to be loved by her would be more spectacular than every wonder of the universe combined.

Erica wiped away her last tear and took a cleansing breath and smiled. "It's really a good thing I'm seeing my therapist tomorrow."

Although Robert had no idea that she had been seeing a therapist, from the lost look he'd just witnessed, he wasn't surprised at all. "What I wouldn't give to be a fly on that wall," he answered back lightly.

Erica laughed musically, and Robert joined in, pulling her tighter to his chest.

"You know, you're wearing too many clothes," Erica said and

sat back to finally remove his polo.

"Thank you," Robert said and purposely filled the words with as much gratitude as he could muster in this moment.

"You're welcome," Erica whispered back and leaned in to return the gratitude with a kiss.

Robert grumbled through their kiss, "I'm still not ready to let you go."

Erica lifted her hips and positioned her opening just over her lover's steel. As she slowly wrapped him in her intimate embrace, she whispered against his lips, "Then don't."

Robert placed Erica's hand over his racing heart, and he placed his over hers as they made love there in the driver's seat of his car. Robert kissed Erica's hot mouth, nibbled her swollen bottom lip and sucked at her tasty tongue. Erica ran her teeth along Robert's strong jaw, licked at the salty sweat on his neck and groaned her pleasure over and over in his ears. She wrapped her arms around him so tightly, and he pulled her as close as he could as their climaxes came. Her chest was pressed against his and their joyous hearts pounded together while the pair's orgasmic cries were swallowed in satiated kisses.

Erica laid back against the steering wheel with her arms behind her head as Robert admired her nakedness in the moonlight, willing this moment to last forever. They had truly had a breakthrough tonight, and he wanted to delve more into what-could-be. However, the storm had moved out, and he could see headlights approaching in the distance.

"I guess we should get moving," he broke the silence.

"I think we've been moving quite well," Erica winked at him, enjoying the lighter mood.

"You know what I mean, Princess. As much as it pains me, we should get dressed, and I should get you home. It's getting late, and people are starting to venture out after the storm."

To punctuate his point, the headlights that were once in the distance zoomed past them.

"Fine," Erica faux-pouted and moved into the passenger seat to start putting on her clothes. "I didn't even get to show you how skilled I was in reverse."

Robert laughed and pulled his boxers and jeans back up, restoring them back to their rightful place before pulling his shirt over his head.

"You're much more fun when you're naked," Erica mused

while running her fingers through her hair.

Robert laughed again and began to turn the ignition. An idea struck him, and he paused. Surprising himself, he looked over at Erica and asked, "Wanna drive?"

Erica's eyes lit up! Even if he had doubted himself a little before that moment, he would let her drive everywhere for the rest of his life if it always made her that happy.

"I think you've proven your skills," he teased and got out of the car to walk around to the passenger side. He opened her door, walked her around and closed her door behind her.

Erica was still repositioning the seat and mirrors when he sat, for the very first time, in the passenger seat of his beloved Camaro.

Erica looked over at him with a grin, started the car, and as she revved the powerful engine winked and said, "Don't worry, Pretty Boy. I'll be gentle."

CHAPTER 20

Erica expertly parallel parked Robert's precious Camaro in front of her apartment building as the last chords to ZZ Top's "Sharp Dressed Man" ended. She and Robert sang pretty much the entire way home, once he loosened up about Erica driving his car. The singing was a nice break from the heavier mood from earlier.

"Look at that," observed Erica. "Not a single scratch, no hint of a burning clutch, and I even parallel parked." Erica sat proudly with a sexy grin.

Robert had to concede. "I am surprised, Princess. Then again, you surprising me should not surprise me."

Erica's grin grew into a smile that went straight to Robert's heart. She looked so carefree. He must let her drive more.

"But, here's something that may surprise you." He could tell he'd piqued Erica's interest. "I told you that no one else had ever driven my car, but you should know that you are the first woman I have ever had sex with in my car. How's that for an honor? Two firsts in one night."

Erica thought it over for a moment. She was, indeed, surprised that he had never had a woman in his car. The car was just plain sexy. It screamed to have wild crazy sex happening on its leather seats.

"Wow, Pretty Boy! I'm honored," she smiled again.

"You should be," he smiled back.

This felt so easy, so right, Robert thought to himself. However, it was getting to be really late, and Monday mornings were always a bitch for him. This one would be worse because he would have to be away from Erica for the first time since Friday night. On top of that, he knew he would have some damage to repair with Ginger if he were ever going to have a relaxed walk to his desk again. He truly had not meant to hurt her feelings. He just didn't expect to meet the woman of his dreams on his date with Ginger. Surely, he could help her understand and that there'd be no hard feelings.

"I'm going to see you to your door. It's almost midnight, and I have work in the morning," he said.

"Oooo, Cinderella has to be home before midnight; huh? Will the

Camaro turn back into a blueberry?" Erica chided.

"Funny, funny, ha ha…because it's blue…I get it" Robert laughed. "Stay there."

Erica was puzzled until she realized that Robert was running around to her side of the car to open her door for her.

"Princess?" he said as he took her hand in his and helped her out of the car.

Erica couldn't help her reply. "I've certainly felt like one this weekend, Pretty Boy. Thank you." She tip-toed to kiss her Prince when her eyes met the stare of a very worried- and angry-looking Brock over Robert's shoulder. "Shit!"

Robert had his eyes closed anticipating her kiss when her *shit* took him by surprise. Opening his eyes to look around, he instantly went on guard. The neighborhood was a good one, but bad things happened even in good neighborhoods.

"Where the hell have you been?! I've been worried sick about you!" a big, booming voice came from behind him.

Robert spun around and saw a wall of muscle running over to Erica. He squared his shoulders and positioned himself between her and the stranger. There was no way in hell anyone was going to get near her, especially with that tone.

Brock stopped in his tracks as soon as he registered Robert's presence.

"Who the hell are you?" the stranger demanded.

Erica spryly stepped between the two large men. She had to diffuse the situation. She decided to start with Brock.

She began quickly in the hopes of calming the men down before fists started flying. "Brock, this is Robert. Robert this is Brock. Brock is a dear friend. Robert is a new friend," Erica began explaining.

Brock looked down at Erica. "I expected to hear from you before now. When you text someone before lunch and tell them that you will text them later, you text them later," Brock chastised Erica. "When I didn't hear from you, I started looking everywhere. With the shit you do…"

"Hey! Who the hell are you to talk to her like that," Robert interrupted and moved to once again stand between Erica and the mountain of a man talking to her like she was a child.

Brock flipped over the badge on the chain hanging mid-chest. "I'm *Detective* Brock Samson," the man asserted. "Erica and I are…*complicated*," he said to define his role in Erica's life.

Complicated. Robert rolled the word around in his brain a few times. Erica never mentioned anyone else, let alone a relationship. The thought of this man and Erica sent his blood boiling.

"The hell we are!" Erica yelled from behind Robert's protectiveness. She stepped between the two men once again and hit Brock across the chest. "We are not complicated, Brock. We are friends," she looked over her shoulder at Robert and finished, "with benefits, yes, but only *friends*." She stressed the word *friends* and hoped Robert understood. He had told her earlier that evening that nothing mattered before Friday, and she was hoping like hell that he really meant that. She adored Brock, but after their conversation in the car and the lovemaking afterward, Erica really wanted to explore whatever she and Robert could be. "Now, both of you, STAND DOWN!"

The weight of the word *friends* seemed to hit Brock harder than Erica's slap across his chest, and his shoulders slumped noticeably. With Brock easing, Robert relaxed his stance a little.

"Brock," Erica softened, "you and I will have lunch tomorrow, and I will fill you in on … whatever *this* is." She tip-toed and kissed him on his cheek, causing Robert to tense again.

Brock closed his eyes and savored the brief brush of Erica's lips on his cheek. Robert could see that the man wanted to be more than friends, and although he knew exactly how he felt and couldn't imagine the pain of being banished to Erica's friend-zone, it took everything he had not to pummel the man.

Robert stuck out his hand to end the confrontation with a gentlemanly handshake, but Brock only stiffened. "Enjoy being her newest Ken Doll for now. You'll be stored away in a quiet corner of her 'Playhouse' soon enough, just like the rest of us," he spat at Robert.

Erica was displeased at Brock's callousness, but she understood his lashing out. She'd let Brock get too close and was now going to have to talk with him…tomorrow.

"Brock!" Erica admonished. "Please, stop. We'll talk tomorrow."

Brock closed his eyes to regain his composure. "Fine. Tomorrow." He looked into Robert's eyes and threatened, "I'll be around."

Robert clenched his jaw to keep from antagonizing the situation any further. The last thing he needed was to be hauled into jail for beating *Detective* Brock Samson's pompous ass. He also didn't want to upset Erica more than this confrontation had already done. Besides, his subconscious was already starting to mull over what Brock meant by his reference to Erica's "Playhouse."

Robert tucked Erica under his arm and led her into the apartment building, not waiting to see if Brock walked away or not. At this point, he didn't care if the man stood there all night. He wasn't leaving her side.

The elevator ride to the top floor had been quiet with both Erica and Robert lost in thought. It was a distinct shift from the playfulness from earlier.

Erica wasn't ready to reveal all to Robert. She wasn't ashamed of her Playhouse or her 'hunting.' Robert had just showed her a whole other side to things this weekend, and she wasn't ready to lift the veil between the two. She'd originally wanted Robert for her next playmate and could envision all of the wonderful sexual activities he would participate in with her and her other playthings. Now, she didn't want to share him with anyone. She couldn't imagine his hands, his mouth or his eyes looking so deeply into anyone else. She wanted to keep Robert and all of his ooey-gooey wonderfulness to herself. She was virtually pouting over the thought of sharing him when the elevator opened to her floor.

Robert stood at Erica's door waiting for her to fish her keys out of her purse. He studied her face as she concentrated on the task of finding the keys and then watched her slender fingers perform the task of unlocking her door. *What was beneath all of that beauty and feistiness?* He stood aside and let Erica walk into the safety of her apartment first and then followed.

Closing the door behind him, he cleared his throat and managed to say, "Are we going to talk about what that was?" Part of him wanted answers, but the other part of him was screaming at him to shut up. *No, we don't want to talk about that! You know there is some messed-up shit here, and we DON'T WANT TO KNOW!*

Erica's eyes pleaded with Robert. "Can we please talk about it tomorrow? Today has been so nice."

Robert considered pushing the subject but decided to give in to her. She had that power over him, and they both knew it. "Okay," he pulled her into his arms. "Tomorrow."

Erica's eyes brightened, "Thank you, Pretty Boy."

"I'm at your service, Princess. You know that," he smiled tentatively, the stress from the confrontation with Brock apparent.

"Do you want to stay the night?" Erica asked hopefully.

Robert considered the question.

"Well, I wasn't because I have work tomorrow, and I don't have anything here. But, after what happened downstairs, I'm damn sure not going to leave you alone for *Brock* to make his way up here and into your bed."

The last part came out as more of an accusation than he's intended, and Robert immediately regretted saying it. The hurt was evident on Erica's face.

"I'm sorry, I didn't mean…"

Fire ripped through Erica. *How dare he?!*

"Yes, you did," Erica held her head up and looked Robert in the eyes. "Because I'm such a whore that I would fuck you all weekend and then invite another man into my bed as soon as you leave."

"Erica, please."

"And why should you believe differently? I invited you and Silicone Bitch up here to fuck both of you and then send you on your way," Erica began crying. "I never should have let you stay."

Robert was cut the core. Not only was Erica crying, but she was crying because he'd hurt her. "Please don't say that. You know that there's something here."

"I *thought* that *maybe* there could be something, that you truly meant it when you said that you didn't care what I had packed away in my baggage, but that was all just some pretty way to fuck me again."

"That's not true, and you know it. Please," Robert reached out to Erica and was rewarded with a sharp slap.

"Get out! Get out! I *never* should have let you stay!"

Robert stood there absorbing the sting from Erica's hand and from her command. There was no way that he was going to leave with the way things were knowing the way things could be *and were going to be*, if he had any say in the matter.

"No," he said simply.

Erica glared at him. "What?"

"I know you're used to getting your way, but not this time. I'm not leaving until you listen to me, accept my apology and let me hold you."

Erica stood there just as shocked as if Robert had hit her back. "No one tells me 'no!'"

"Well, I did. I am. Get used to it because I'm not leaving," Robert punctuated his intent by walking across the living room and sinking into her luxurious leather sofa.

Erica growled, locked the door and stormed down the hall. A moment later, Robert heard a door slam shut.

Robert took his shoes off and stretched out across the leather.

Tonight was going to be a long night.

CHAPTER 21

Erica lay awake in the middle of her bed. This wasn't her playroom bed of red satin and handy leather cuffs at each post. That room was where she played and entertained. That bed was where she was Mistress Erica, Queen of the Debauched.

This bed, in this room, was her sanctuary. The four-poster canopy was covered in pink 1,000-thread-count Egyptian cotton sheets and topped by a soft pink down comforter. Grey, cream and pink pillows piled high, and the entire sanctum was draped in pink gossamer. All of the furniture surrounding the bed was white with silver trim, and the accompanying décor proclaimed her femininity. No one had ever been invited over its threshold. Here, Erica could be herself. It was such a stark contrast to her playroom, just as the woman she was in this room was different from the woman everyone saw – everyone except *him*.

She couldn't believe that the man who had treated her so kindly over the weekend, the man who had just introduced her to his mother, could have lashed out like he did. The gall of him thinking that she would invite Brock to her bed after such a weekend – such a wonderful, fun weekend, the kind of weekend that could make her believe in happily-ever-afters again. Spending the day with Robert's family and then having the conversation they'd had in the car between some of the most wonderful sex she'd had since the last time they'd had sex had made an impression on her protected heart. John Foster may have weakened the fortress by making Erica see that men could truly honor and love women, but Robert had started removing stones, piece by piece, exposing her need to love and to be loved.

Then, to top it off, he'd told her no! Erica tossed from her side to her back and started up at the top of her canopy. How he infuriated her! Not only did he hurt her, but he defied her, too. *How dare he,* she thought for the thousandth time since she'd slammed her bedroom door to leave him alone on her couch. That was four hours ago - four hours of fuming, thinking and trying to will herself to sleep. She'd tried everything: counting, reciting poetry, making lists, saying the alphabet over and over. Nothing had worked.

Erica took a deep breath and sat up in bed. Surely, he'd given up and gone. Besides, he had to work in a few hours, and he himself had said that he had nothing here. *Nothing here*. She knew that he'd meant things like deodorant and clean clothes, but after the turn the night had taken, *nothing here* felt like it meant so much more.

Sounds from her kitchen illuminated Erica's way back from the dark path her thoughts were taking. Fury, confusion and excitement mixed in her belly and sent her flying out of bed. She was furious that Robert was still here. The next instant, she wondered why he was still here, but by the time she reached the door to her room, she was filled with such relief that he was still here that she couldn't wait to see him – just to see if he was real. Still, she calmed herself before opening her door and tiptoeing out into the hall.

The journey to the end of her hall seemed to take a lifetime as Erica crept slowly, trying to calm the pounding of her heart. She closed her eyes as she reached her destination. *Please, let him be there. Please, let him be there. Please, let him be there.* She felt like Dorothy clicking her heels together three times and wishing to go home, but if it worked, that's all that would matter.

Erica opened her eyes and stood inches away from her wish. The heat from his body as he stood there in only his boxers radiated through her white, satin gown and warmed her skin. *Oh, he feels so good!* Relief hit her so hard that were it not for the gravity of his body holding her in place, she probably would have fallen.

"Hi," Robert was the first to break the silence.

"Hi," Erica whispered back.

"I hope I didn't wake you," he offered. "I was just getting some water."

Erica started to put on her armor and tell him that yes, he did wake her and that she wished he would have gone home, but looking up into his tired face, she could see the worry in his eyes.

"You didn't wake me," she said truthfully. "I couldn't sleep."

Robert ran a hand over his face. "Yeah, me, either. Listen, can we please talk *now*?"

Erica stood silent for a moment. They did need to talk, but it wasn't going to be in the hallway. She had just the perfect place.

Grabbing Robert by the hand, she said, "Let's go."

Robert's surprise rooted him in place, and he tugged Erica back. The question shone in his eyes, and Erica understood immediately.

"You said you wanted me to listen to you, accept your apology, and then you would hold me. Well, I promise to listen. I accept your apology, so we're skipping ahead to the 'holding me' part," she explained.

Robert took Erica's lead and followed her down the hall. Thinking that they were headed to the last room on the right, he almost knocked her over when she stopped one door shy.

Erica grasped the doorknob, paused and then turned to look at Robert.

"Just so you know, no one – *I mean no one* – has ever accompanied me into this room. This is *mine*. Spending just a little time with me but seeing through me the way you do, seeing me broken in your car earlier this evening, please tell me that you understand the importance of me letting you in."

Robert's eyes moistened, and he nodded his head silently both in answer to her question and in a reverent prayer of thanks.

Erica was letting him in.

CHAPTER 22

Robert curled around Erica in the middle of her haven. As she relaxed into him, he couldn't help looking around the room and think that this room was perfect for his Princess. A soft lamp illuminated crystals, silver and all of the things that told him how soft, vulnerable and sweet Erica was – all things he knew already.

Her satin-covered body tensed when he broke their silence.

"Are you going to tell me what Brock meant tonight by calling me just another Ken Doll for your Playhouse?"

Erica turned over in his arms and looked into his eyes.

"Yes, but first, I want to tell you a story. I need you to understand why I am the way that I am, why I invite couples back here to have sex and what led me to you," Erica confessed. "*If* you still want to be here after that, then I will not only tell you about my house, I will show it to you. Will you please listen?"

Robert couldn't imagine anything that would make him leave Erica. He knew that she was broken, that there was some great pain in her past, but none of that mattered to him. Of course, he needed to control his temper better and not say things to hurt her or to condemn her for her past, and he would do much better about that. He never wanted to make her cry again.

"Before you begin," Robert pleaded, "please know that I am truly sorry for what I said tonight. I was angry at Brock, confused by so many things and completely taken by surprise by how deeply I feel for you. My remark was shitty and uncalled for, and I'm sorry."

Robert reached up and brushed a bramble of Erica's untamed curls from her shoulder.

"And know that no matter what you tell me, no matter what you show me, I'll still be right here," he finished his plea.

"Be careful what you promise, Pretty Boy."

Robert pulled Erica closer to his warmth and kissed her slowly. In that kiss, he endeavored to pour all of his understanding, all of his patience and all of his acceptance. He tried to tell her with that one kiss that he loved her. He hoped that she would feel his love because they were words that she wasn't quite ready to hear.

Seeming to understand, Erica broke the kiss and turned away from Robert. With her back to his front and their pajamas between them, Erica pulled Robert's arm over her like a shield and began her story.

"I was in love once," she began. "Oh, it was as 'in love' as a 17-year-old could be, but I was. I could see our whole life – wedding, kids, growing old together. I had cast him in the role of my Prince Charming, and I was his Princess."

Robert tightened his grasp and pulled her closer to him at the mention of "Princess." The tone in her voice as she told him the beginning of her story reminded him of a dark, distorted fairytale as told by Stephen King or Charles Campbell. He wasn't sure exactly where she was going, but he knew right away that there would be no happy ending.

"His name was Kurt. We were high-school sweethearts, prom royalty and the most beautiful of the beautiful people. Of course, having the perfect fairytale wedding in mind, I was saving myself for the perfect wedding night – just like Cinderella and Prince Charming. One night, senior year, after he had taken our football team to the championships and won, he asked me to meet him in the middle of the football field. I was so excited! It was going to be a perfect proposal."

Robert cringed at the way Erica punctuated "perfect." She filled it with venom, like the Evil Queen poisoned the apple for Snow White.

"The stench from cheap beer permeated his skin, and he grabbed at me. I told him over and over again that he was hurting me, but he didn't hear me. All he kept saying was how beautiful I was and how much he loved me and wanted to feel me."

"Stop, please," Robert interrupted and squeezed her tightly. It was so tight that it should have been uncomfortable, but, to Erica, it felt safe. "You don't have to tell me what happened."

Erica rubbed his arm with her hand to reassure him that she was okay and relished in the strength stretched beneath his skin. He was so strong.

"No, I guess I don't. Needless to say, I was shattered. I was humiliated, and I felt so stupid. There were no such things as fairytales or princes. There were no happily-ever-afters, not for me, anyway. He had seen to that. I wasn't worthy. He had stolen my innocence, in more ways than one."

Anger ripped through Robert. "Tell me he paid for what he did to you!"

Erica sighed. "In a way. It was the hardest thing I ever had to do, but I told Daddy. Daddy wanted to save me from being publically humiliated. He found me a doctor to make sure that I was okay and not pregnant, even though I assured him that the asshole had fumbled with a condom. Then Daddy had a meeting with his father and threatened to destroy the boy's future and squash any hopes of an ivy-league scholarship. To drive the point home, Daddy told the man that he would make sure that everybody who was anybody in this town would know that his son was a rapist, and he would be financially ruined. His family moved after that. I never knew where. I didn't care to know."

Robert liked her father immediately. "Wow. Your dad?" he asked realizing that he had no idea about her family.

"Randolph Spencer," Erica said proudly.

"*The* Randolph Spencer? The man who owns more than half of this town and the next?" Robert asked, quite impressed. Randolph Spencer not only owned most of the property in town, but he also had the reputation for being a ruthless businessman. He held controlling interest in several businesses and was senior partner of Spencer,

Tucker, Johnson, CPA. Working for the best marketing firm in the region, Robert had actually helped on a few campaigns for Spencer; he'd even seen the man at a few marketing functions. He knew that Randolph Spencer was quite formidable. He could also see where Erica got her feistiness, her sense of entitlement and her backbone.

"That's my Daddy," Erica said again and smiled. Erica did love her father. He had defended her and protected her. If she delved deeper into the way his spoiling increased after the incident, she would have known that he'd felt senseless guilt over the pain his only child, his daughter, had gone through and his powerlessness to take it from her.

"So, fast-forward a few weeks. I kept replaying the incident over and over in my mind, and one thing kept coming to me. Kurt and I had been all alone. There had been no one in the stands, no cheerleaders on the sidelines, no players around us. If there had been people around, it would never have happened. Then it clicked to me: There was safety in numbers. I mean, you hear it all your life from your parents and from teachers. 'Don't walk home alone. There is safety in numbers.' All of those warnings came back to me, and I thought, 'Don't be alone with a boy. There is safety in numbers.'

After graduating and trying my hand at college, I noticed the way boys – and girls, for that matter – looked at me. Oh, I hadn't dared be with anyone after that night on the football field, but I'd noticed. The lower-cut my blouse, the extra whipped cream on my mocha. The shorter my skirt, the more leniencies on my lackluster answers to my essay questions. I couldn't trust anyone to be alone with them, but I did love the power my body seemed to hold over people. One night, I was at a party with some classmates, and a guy and his girlfriend approached me. He was horny, and she was curious. He'd talked her into a threesome, and they both thought I was hot. I tried it and felt safe and realized that this whole sex thing was quite powerful. *Voila!* Mistress Erica was born."

A lot of things started making sense to Robert: her approaching him and Ginger in the club, her initial refusal to have one-on-one sex after Ginger had gone.

"But you don't always have sex with multiple partners. I mean, I'm proof," Robert interrupted.

"No, not always, but it takes a deep amount of trust that is not so easily earned," Erica turned back over to look at Robert. "Which is why you took me so off guard."

Robert kissed her lightly. "I'm so glad that I did."

Erica sighed, "Me, too, Pretty Boy. Me, too."

"So, you told me *how*, and I'm still here. I'm not loosening my grip on you, and I'm not running for the door," Robert encouraged Erica to continue.

"It's almost 5am. Aren't you exhausted?" Erica asked.

"Absolutely, but I want to know you, everything about you. Please, your house?"

Erica took a deep breath.

"I lined up a few people that I enjoyed having sex with. There was no commitment involved, and we had a lot of fun. We got tired of shuffling from place to place each time we wanted to get together, so I bought a house out in the country, away from prying eyes. We all get together a couple times a month and have, kind of a," Erica didn't know another way to explain it, "sex party."

Robert's eyes grew wide.

"Imagine every fantasy you've ever wanted and multiply it by ten, and that's what happens at the house, my Playhouse, so to speak."

"And your playmates?" Robert asked referencing Brock's warning from earlier.

"Some people grow weary and stop coming to the group. Others move away. So, I go to the club – my club, by the way – and seek new couples to add. We come back to my playroom here, and I take them for a trial run. If I'm impressed, I invite them to my house."

"Wait a minute? *Your* club?" Robert asked.

"I tell you I host sex parties at my house in the country, and you focus on the part about the club? Yes, *my* club. I own it and several other businesses in town. Daddy doesn't *completely* support me.

Anyway, if I have taken particular interest in a member of our party, then I will have sex with them one-on-one. I've seen that they can be trusted with the way they treat the others, so I can indulge in one-on-one sex. The house is my way of having the sex that I have grown to crave and still find some type of intimacy in a private setting. It's my way of *screening* partners, I guess."

Erica paused. She knew bringing up Brock's name was going to be unpleasant, but she needed Robert to know everything.

"That's where Brock comes in," Erica began.

Robert closed his eyes and breathed in the sweet smell of her hair. It was calming to him, and more than anything right now, he needed calm.

"Brock was originally part of a package deal that split up. Because he was fun and kind and respectful, he'd become a favorite of the house, so he kept coming around. Seeing that he could be trusted, I invited him to my private room. Sometimes there was sex. Other times it was cards or silly TV or just easy conversation. He became my friend," Erica explained.

"You know he wants more," Robert interjected. "I could see that tonight when you kissed his cheek. It was painful, the look on his face, I mean."

Erica sighed again.

"I know he wants more, and I try to be careful with him. I adore him. I trust him. I feel safe with him, but there's something missing," Erica explained.

Robert swallowed and nodded. Erica saw the relief in his eyes and felt him relax with the acceptance of the fact that she and Brock were only friends.

Robert thought this over. "And Ginger and I were?"

"Gorgeous! Oh my God!" Erica's eyes lit up. "I wanted you both so bad, but I was drawn to you. I wanted to have you. I wanted to add you to my group. I wanted you to prove to me that you could be trusted so that I could roll around with you, and I was going to show you so many wonders and share so many pleasures with you as a reward."

"So, I was going to be added to your *collection*?" Robert asked, not particularly liking the way that made him feel.

"Well, yes, at first," Erica answered matter-of-factly. "But Ginger messed that up. Then you *really* messed it up by being so…" Erica hunted for the right word before settling on, "wonderful."

Robert warmed a little at her praise but still felt uneasy about the house and Erica's sex parties. Though the idea of a threesome – or more – was appealing in fantasy, he knew without a doubt that he could not share Erica. He hoped that she felt the same about him.

"Now that you've told me about the house, will you show me?" Robert asked. He needed to see this to make it real.

Erica was uneasy about revealing the depth of her depravity to Robert. She explained to him why she did what she did, but she was still afraid of being judged by the man who made her feel so far removed from that life, who made her feel like she was worthy of so much more. She also knew that, while the thought of sharing Robert with Di and Sky originally turned her on, it sickened her now.

"I told you I would, and I will. There's a party Friday, and we'll go," Erica said flatly. "I need to make an appearance anyway."

"Friday," Robert echoed. "Okay."

Erica turned away from Robert so that he couldn't see the tears forming behind her eyes. She didn't realize until that moment that she didn't want that world to invade the world she and Robert had created this weekend. It was too perfect for real life to spoil.

Robert was chilled by a thought that should have driven him crazy with lust. A sex party with a sexy woman whom he happened to be crazy about was quite a fantasy, but something in his gut simmered with dread. He pulled Erica's body closer to his and buried his face in her hair hoping to fill his body with every essence of hers.

Monday had arrived, and real life waited on the other side of the alarm clock.

CHAPTER 23

Robert grabbed the bouquet of fall flowers extra-tight and put on his best smile as he strolled toward the reception desk where Ginger sat with a firm scowl. The cellophane wrapped around the stems crinkled in his grip and seemed to echo louder than he knew was realistically possible, announcing to the world that he had an apology to make to the buxom blonde at the desk. He'd stopped at a 24-hour grocery on the way to work this morning and grabbed them in an effort to show Ginger that he wasn't the horrible person she must think him to be. He honestly had had every intention of spending the night rolling around with her in what he had hoped would develop into a beautiful friendship with an excellent benefits package. How could he have known how drastically his life would have changed that night?

Robert reached the reception desk and presented the flowers to

Ginger.

"For you, to apologize," he offered sincerely.

Ginger's steel stare softened as she reached for the flowers.

"Thank you," she whispered. "You didn't have to."

"I *wanted* to," Robert answered truthfully. "I really did have a great time with you Friday night. It was more fun than I'd had in a very long time."

Ginger leaned closer across the desk to whisper to Robert out of earshot of their arriving co-workers. To the casual onlooker, the pretty pair bent over the bouquet of flowers looked cozy and romantic, a stolen moment between lovers at the beginning of their workday.

It was anything but.

"Then why did you put me in a cab to go home *alone*?" Ginger asked with genuine curiosity. "Could I have done anything differently … other than stay with you and *her*?"

The smell of her perfume was too sweet as it mixed with the flowers and was making Robert's head start to spin. This was a conversation that could not be had here in the middle of reception with an unclear head.

Robert answered as truthfully as he could without hurting

Ginger's feelings. Underneath all of the makeup and silicone, she really was a sweet girl.

"It's … complicated, and, no. I had to stay." Robert squared his jaw, swallowed and kept the truth flowing. He didn't want to let Ginger think that there would be a second date to follow the flowers. "You are a very sweet girl, and I had a great time. It's just that there was … something … there that I had to see through."

Ginger's eyes misted.

"And did you, *see it through?*"

Robert nodded.

Ginger looked down at her flowers.

"I see. So, you and me …"

"… are co-workers who went to dinner and had fun dancing, who made each other laugh and had a really great time," Robert finished.

The tear that escaped Ginger's expertly painted eye sliced into Robert's heart. He hated to see a woman cry. He especially hated it when he was the reason for her tears. Robert reached across the top of the desk and grabbed a tissue to catch Ginger's tear.

He tried to comfort her as best as he could without giving her false hope.

"No tears over me, please," he chuckled. "You give me much more credit than I'm worth."

Ginger dabbed the edges of both eyes and softly said, "I think you're pretty great."

Another path, another life, and he could have taken Ginger in his arms and kissed her tears away. This was not that life, and the only path he cared about led right back to Erica. He said the only thing he could to make her feel better, "I think you're pretty great, too."

That got a smile from Ginger, and she wiped her tears quickly before tossing the tissue in the wastebasket at her feet.

"I need to get these in water," she said brightly. "Thank you for the date, the apology and the flowers, Handsome."

Robert smiled with relief. "So we're …"

"… Okay," it was Ginger's turn to finish his sentence. "Yes, we're fine. Now, go to work before Mr. Treat hunts you down to see the progress you've made on those melons."

This time, Robert laughed as he remembered the work on the fine melons at Andrew's Farm that awaited him this morning.

"Thank you, Ginger," he said sincerely.

She smiled and shooed him down the hall toward his desk.

Robert felt the weight lift from his shoulders. Still, nothing could alleviate the unease that was growing in his stomach. He just hoped the day would pass quickly so that he could get back to Erica.

The morning had been excruciating. He'd only gotten a couple of hours sleep over the course of the entire night. The night had begun beautifully in his car after a trip to his mother's. The sex had been wonderful. With Erica, he knew that it always would be. It was the crack in Erica's defenses that made the night so great. She opened up a little in the car, but after their fight, she'd opened up completely. He knew the enormity of what she'd done, both in inviting him in to her private bedroom and in telling him so much about her life. He knew that he'd held the true Erica last night, the Erica the rest of the world had never met, the Erica behind the smart mouth and barbed tongue. He also knew with every fiber of his being that he needed to hold her again, to make love to her, to kiss away her insecurities and help bandage her wounds so that they could heal instead of building a future on top of them. He couldn't do that sitting at his desk, but work was a necessity for him, so he began with hopes that the day would pass quickly.

CHAPTER 24

Erica sat across from Brock in their favorite downtown restaurant. She was picking through her steak salad while he devoured his bison burger.

"So, are you going to tell me about *Robert*?" Brock growled between bites of his burger.

Erica put her fork down, pulled her napkin out of her lap and set it on the table. Pushing her half-empty plate away, she crossed her arms in front of her to prepare for the upcoming conversation. Though she kept men at arm's length – *until Robert*, she reminded herself – Brock had gotten close. She genuinely liked him and enjoyed spending time with him. However, he'd made it quite clear on more than one occasion that he wanted to be much more than friends. Erica liked to think that she had that much pull on him, but she knew that he was still in love with his hard-headed wife and that one day the hard-headed detective sitting across from her would figure that out. She did not relish hurting his feelings, but she knew that this was all part of Brock's journey to his happily-ever-after.

"Robert is complicated," Erica began.

"That's funny," Brock interrupted. "Last night, I thought that *we* were complicated."

Erica narrowed her blue eyes at her lunch companion.

"Are you going to let me finish?"

Brock put his hands up in mock-surrender and urged her to continue.

"I went out Friday, just like I said I was going to do. I was getting ready to leave the club empty-handed when in walked Robert with a gorgeous, silicone-DD blonde."

Brock's eyes got wide. Erica knew how he loved big boobs, fake or not. She grinned at her friend. The playfulness in his eyes reminded her of his kindness, which is one of the main qualities that brought him to her bed.

"I know. You love boobs, you boob!" she teased her friend.

"What's not to love? They're all round and soft and pretty. You know. You've seen them," Brock teased back.

With a smirk, Erica agreed, "Yes, I have, and you are not wrong."

With that, they laughed with the comfort of old friends, which is why Erica hated to hurt Brock. She stopped laughing, and Brock took a long sip of his sweet tea.

"He's different," Brock broke their silence.

Erica nodded.

"Very."

"How?"

Erica shook her head back and forth slowly before shrugging her shoulders.

"I don't know. He just is."

Brock snorted in derision. "Bullshit! That's a copout, and you know it."

Erica dropped her voice an octave before continuing, "I have never lied to you."

Brock took notice of her tone. Playful-Erica was gone. Sitting before him was Mistress Erica, and she never lied and never sugar-coated things.

Brock shook his head.

"Well, I'll be damned," he said in disbelief. "So what? Do you love him?"

The question shocked Erica, but she wasn't sure why. She'd thought the L-word in her head several times since waking up next to Robert Saturday morning, but saying it out loud was unimaginable.

"Um – I don't know," she answered honestly.

"Shit, Erica. Really?"

"What?" Erica answered innocently.

"*He's* the one who got through? I've been trying for months to make you have the same look on your face that you do right now. Dammit!" Brock slammed his fists on the table, drawing attention from the other diners.

"Brock, control your shit!" Erica shot back at him, not caring about what the onlookers thought.

Brock looked around and offered nods of apology and waited for the restaurant's patrons to get back to their conversations.

"I'm sorry, but you have to know how I feel about you," his voice was laced with the pain he was feeling.

Dammit, Robert! Erica thought to herself. He'd not only chipped away at the wall she'd built around her heart, but he'd apparently broken that bastard all the way down because she felt Brock's pain straight through to her core. It hit her in the stomach like a sneaky sucker punch. Erica wasn't an evil person before; her conscious would allow her to feel bad if warranted, but this was so much more powerful than a little guilt.

Erica nodded that she did, indeed, know how Brock felt about her and added, "I do, Brock. That's why this has to stop."

Horror shot across his handsome face at Erica's rejection.

"Erica, no! You just met this guy," Brock's voice shook with barely-restrained emotion.

Erica stretched her arm across the table and put a comforting hand over Brock's. Hers was so small against his, but it seemed to work a little. Brock's big frame relaxed into her touch.

"I have to see where this leads," Erica said. "I'm going to show him everything, warts and all. Then I'll know. But in the meantime," she stroked his arm slowly, "I can't keep hurting you. You mean too much to me."

She offered Brock a small smile, and he smiled weakly back.

"You know I'm going to keep an eye on you," Brock threatened.

Erica grinned at her friend, "I wouldn't expect anything less. Besides, you know the shit I'm in to. I need a bodyguard."

Brock laughed sadly.

"I won't come back to the house," he said finally.

Erica frowned and then nodded in understanding. She'd gotten used to his boisterous energy and booming laughter throughout the house.

"You will be missed," she said sadly, knowing that she would miss him so much.

He nodded and then motioned for the check. When their server came, Erica beat him to it.

"There's no way you're paying after this," she said.

Brock smiled at her.

"At least let me leave the tip," he bargained.

Erica shook her head.

"No. I'll take care of this tip, and I'll give you one."

Brock tilted his head to the side, grinned and waited on Erica's words of wisdom.

"Go visit your ex-wife. A beautiful lady, wise beyond her years, told me that once you've had that once-in-a-lifetime love, nothing else compares. I don't know what this is with Robert, but if you feel even a tenth of it for your ex, then you owe it to both of you to go back and at least try to work things out," Erica said, suddenly sounding years older and infinitely wiser.

Brock sat there, absolutely stunned.

Erica handed the server enough cash to cover their bill and a generous tip, kissed Brock on the cheek and walked out of the downtown bistro.

CHAPTER 25

"Thank God you could see me on such short notice," Erica flew into Dr. Boyd's office without preamble. She tossed her purse on the floor next to the couch and kicked her feet up on the ottoman.

"Well, hello, to you, too, Erica," Dr. Boyd said cheerfully. "Did something happen over the weekend?"

Erica looked at her therapist. She looked different today. She was prettier, and her glasses must have been replaced with contacts. There was a blush to her cheeks, and her auburn hair that was usually tied up severely behind her head rested in soft waves on her shoulders.

Erica said slyly, "I don't know, you tell me. You look...*different.*"

"This is not *my* therapy session. This is yours," Dr. Boyd expertly rounded the conversation back to her patient.

Erica conceded. She did need to talk.

"Yes! Dammit! Something happened!" Erica spat.

Dr. Boyd studied Erica for a moment before proceeding with caution.

"Your tone says that the something was bad, but I get the feeling that it is something else entirely. Tell me about it," she grabbed her legal pad and pen, sat down in the worn leather chair across from Erica and started jotting notes.

Erica growled.

"Fine," Erica took a deep breath. "I met someone."

The pretty therapist looked up from her notes.

"Oh! Do tell," she prodded Erica.

Nervous energy coursed through Erica, and she had to get up to walk it off as she told Dr. Boyd the story of how she'd met Robert and every detail of their incredible weekend together, including her spilling her guts all over her pretty pink Egyptian cotton sheets.

Erica finished her story behind the doctor's desk, and her eyes got wide. Erica laughed.

"Daddy thought that sending me to a female therapist would keep me from seducing another one," she laughed.

Dr. Boyd stood up and faced Erica.

"You bat for my team!" Erica said while holding up a photo of her therapist with another pretty woman. They were both wearing white suits on what was obviously their wedding day.

Dr. Boyd smiled back at Erica.

"That's where you're wrong, Erica. You see, you are just another pretty face in the crowd to me. The world is full of them. What you're seeing in that picture, that's love. As far as I'm concerned, she is the only woman in the world."

The doctor's words were full of fire and passion, and Erica had no doubt. She even felt a little foolish standing there thinking that there was any moment Dr. Boyd had been attracted to her.

Erica was so moved by the declaration that she wanted to hear more.

"Will you tell me about her?" Erica genuinely asked.

"Because you seem quite genuine and because you shared, I'll give you the abbreviated version. We met in college. She went into medicine, and I went into psychology. She's head of the emergency room here at the hospital. We have a wonderful marriage," she added. "Now, that's all you'll get out of me about my personal life. Let's talk about you and Robert, this weekend and what you're feeling."

Erica sat back down and felt much calmer.

"I don't know what I'm feeling," Erica said after a while of silent introspection.

"Okay. So, just rattle off some things you felt this weekend," the therapist guided her.

Erica pursed her lips together. Feeling something was one thing. Admitting to feeling it was something else entirely.

"Erica, you don't have to be afraid," Dr. Boyd began.

"But that's just it. I *am* afraid. I am absolutely, fucking petrified!" Erica shouted as her dam erupted inside. "I'm afraid that I love him. I'm afraid that he loves me. I'm afraid that he's going to hurt me. I'm afraid that he's going to see who I really am and leave and … and … and then what? What do I do? He's made me feel like I am worth something, worth being loved, but if he sees what that something really is, how irrevocably broken I am, what if he leaves?"

Dr. Boyd finished making some notes and let Erica catch her breath.

"Erica, honey, you *are* worth loving. You always have been. You had something awful happen to you at an early age, and you chose to deal with it unconventionally. No one can judge you. People don't

205

know how they will process and deal with something tragic until, God forbid, it happens to them. Just because you've chosen to live a certain lifestyle doesn't mean you can't love or be loved."

Dr. Boyd paused for effect and let Erica process her words.

"It sounds like Robert gives you what you thought you were looking for with John," she finished.

Erica fidgeted.

"Fuck! I knew you were right," she said dramatically and sank deeper into her chair.

Dr. Boyd smirked, "So did I, my dear. So did I."

"Bitch," Erica said playfully.

"Indeed," Dr. Boyd answered back and jotted more notes into her pad.

After a few more moments of silence, Erica began talking again.

"I have to show him the house," she admitted.

"Oh?" Dr. Boyd asked. "What brought this about?"

Erica recalled the near-fight between Brock and Robert and the train wreck that happened afterward, including his refusal to leave and her not only telling him about the house and how it came to be, but also that she promised to show him Friday.

"And how does that make you feel?" the therapist asked.

"Really, Doc? The stereotypical 'and how does that make you feel?' "

Dr. Boyd shrugged.

"Sometimes the classics work," she smirked.

"Really? The classics," Erica acquiesced. "Fine. Again, it makes me feel scared."

"Scared of what?"

"Scared of how Robert will react. Scared of what he will think of me. Scared of what he will want," Erica admitted.

"What he will want?" Erica could tell that she found this interesting.

"Well, I did pick him up in a bar and brought him back to my apartment to have a *ménage*. What if he wants that there? Now?"

"And if he does? Could you go through with it?" her therapist asked.

Erica knew the answer but didn't want to admit it. Admitting it was too close to declaring something for Robert that she wasn't ready to declare.

"Erica, you can tell me. It doesn't leave this room. You're already feeling it. Saying it won't change things," Dr. Boyd encouraged.

Erica took a deep breath, filled up her lungs with courage and said, finally, "I couldn't go through with it." She lowered her head in defeat.

"Erica, look at me," Dr. Boyd soothed.

Erica looked up.

"Admitting that you feel so much for this man that you don't want to share him is not defeat. It's not weak. It's strong. It's a victory. It's a wonderful thing."

Erica looked at her doubtfully, and a sob caught in her throat.

"Don't you see? You have finally found what you have been searching for all your life. You needed someone to love who also loves you back. From what you've told me, this man does. You've won, my dear. Open your heart and claim your happiness."

The tears broke free from Erica and years of self-doubt washed away. She cried for the next half hour in Dr. Boyd's office.

She cried because she was happy.

She cried because she felt free.

She cried because she was in love, but most of all, she cried for something she never thought would happen.

She cried because she was loved.

CHAPTER 26

Erica rushed to the door to her apartment and flung it open.

"It took you long enough to get here," she said to Robert and threw herself into his arms. After the visit with Dr. Boyd this afternoon, that statement meant so much more to Erica. It had taken a lifetime for Robert to arrive. He was the Prince in all of her childhood fairytales. He was the Knight-in-Shining-Armor that slayed dragons and wore her favors into battle, and he'd certainly had to battle. He'd had to fight to convince her to let him stay Friday night after the debacle with the failed threesome. He'd had to fight to stay the weekend, take her to his mother's home and then again, to stay after the argument late Sunday night after Brock's unexpected visit. It was time that the brave knight got his princess.

Robert threw his overnight bag across the threshold before

wrapping his arms around her tiny body. He pulled her close for a moment before stepping back to take a look at Erica. He was nervous about meeting her here after work after the fight the night before and her confessions that followed. She *looked* like the Erica he left that morning, though he could tell that she'd been crying – a lot. He needed to know what had made her cry, but first, he needed to get her behind closed doors. He'd spent more time away from her today than he could stand, and the need to kiss her was overwhelming.

Without speaking, Robert slid one hand from Erica's arm down her back, over the ample curve of her bottom and scooped her up effortlessly into his arms. He quickly carried her into her apartment and pulled the door shut behind them with his foot.

Erica squealed. *She was free!* In Robert's arms, she was weightless, carefree and happy.

"What are you –," Erica began.

Robert cut her off by crushing his lips to hers in the kiss the he'd been craving all day. She was his drug, his sustenance and his nourishment. Her breath filled every fiber of his body. Her fire kept him warm. Her eyes kept him grounded. Her heart was his rhythm. He'd been lonely for so long. He'd searched for love and had even though that he'd found it with Amelia.

Robert had been nearly convinced of his heart's intentions before leaving for work this morning, but it was in being away from Erica all day, coming here to find her waiting for him, holding her in his arms after longing for her all day, that he truly knew how he felt.

He loved Erica.

Robert carried Erica to the couch and sat down with her still cradled in his arms locked in an insatiable kiss.

"You," kiss. "Seem," kiss. "Happy," kiss. "To," kiss. "See," kiss. "Me," kiss. Erica said between kisses.

"MmmmHmmm," Robert murmured in response, never breaking the kiss.

"Are," kiss. "You," kiss. "Hungry?" kiss. Erica asked.

"MmmmHmmm," was Robert's response, again not taking his lips off hers.

Erica giggled, which only made Robert kiss her harder.

"For," kiss. "Food?" kiss. Erica giggled again.

"Later," Robert groaned into her mouth.

Erica growled her response and wriggled to sit in her lover's lap. She was starving for him as she ripped his white Oxford shirt open, sending buttons flying. She leaned back to admire her work and grinned. Robert's succulent lips were swollen with her kisses, and his deep blue eyes were dark with desire. She ground her hips into his lap, dug her nails into his chest and bit into his neck. The flesh was salty and sweet, and his manly fragrance fueled her hunger for him. The combination of the way he felt, the way he tasted and the way he smelled made Erica almost rabid with want.

Robert couldn't think. All he could do was feel and experience the force of nature on his lap. Her teeth in his neck and her nails on his chest made him rock solid with his need for her. Seeing her fiery hair splayed down her back as she bent to bite him combined with the fire burning his body at every point of contact. He desperately wanted to be consumed.

He ripped at the flimsy blouse keeping him from Erica's creamy skin. It fell apart in the force of his fists, and he tossed it to the floor. One skillful hand freed the clasp from her bra, and he discarded it on the growing pile of ruined clothing.

Erica tossed her head back and thrust her breasts into Robert's large hands. He squeezed both with such force that Erica moaned and ground against his lap once more. He pulled her by the breasts to his hungry mouth and took turns biting and pinching, pinching and biting her sensitive buds, all the while her nipples were screaming for more. Erica was a bundle of sensation on Robert's lap, even though they were still clothed from the waist down.

Robert broke his kiss from Erica's breast and found her mouth once more, but he let her know that he wasn't finished with her bountiful mounds. He rolled both nipples between his thumbs and forefingers, gradually increasing the pressure, as his mouth explored hers in the hungriest kiss. Taking her swollen lower lip between his teeth, he bit hard while squeezing and pulling both nipples.

Every pinch, every bite, every exquisite moment of pain sent pleasure shooting through her body to her pussy, still covered by her jeans and separated from Robert's need. He was going to make her come just by torturing her with his hands and teeth, and Erica was thrilled! Her pleasure was his sole focus, and that thought mixed with his ministrations drove her over the edge. The next hard pinch on her raw nipples ignited the orgasm that rocketed through her body and escaped in screams that Robert swallowed with his kisses.

As her orgasm faded, Robert eased from pinching to a loving caress of her full breasts. His kiss softened to gratitude as he pulled her tight to his chest and shifted until he was lying on top of her on the leather couch that he had spent most of the night. He broke their kiss long enough to remove the offending clothes still remaining and, always careful of her tiny frame, gently laid back on top of Erica to once again find her lips.

Erica could feel the heat from his cock as it rested just outside her dripping opening. She'd just had an orgasm, but she needed Robert inside of her. She grabbed a handful of his curly black hair and pulled him away from her lips. She begged him with her eyes to take away her need.

Robert answered and slowly slid inside of Erica. She was so hot and wet that he almost came then and there, but once he was completely sheathed, he stilled and caught his breath. Looking down at Erica, eyes closed and breathing deeply, his heart swelled with the depth of his feelings for her. He'd fallen fast and hard for the redheaded nymph beneath him.

"Is there something wrong?" Erica asked opening her eyes.

Robert smiled down at her.

"Absolutely nothing, Princess," Robert answered and kissed her softly.

He began moving slowly in and out, savoring each moment of the friction created by their bodies. Erica's body arched into his so perfectly leaving an opening for him to wrap his strong arms underneath her back and pull her into him.

"You are my heaven," Robert breathed against her cheek as he pushed inside her again.

"Robert, I…" Erica broke off and closed her eyes as he entered her again.

Robert rocked back and forth into his lover's body relishing the feeling of her body welcoming him, the feeling of her widening to accept his length and closing behind him as he withdrew. Her body, so small but firm and supple, felt like it was made just for him.

"Robert, ppplllleeeaaasssseee," Erica begged.

He gave her what she needed and sped up, thrusting faster, pushing her toward another orgasm. The way their bodies fit, he could feel her swollen clit rubbing against his shaft as he pushed faster into her body.

"Come on, Princess. Again. Come for me again, Beautiful," Robert commanded.

Erica's body tensed and arched high into his. He could feel

each spasm of her orgasm massaging him toward his. Her moans were music to his ears; like the Pied Piper, she led him over the cliff with her, and he kissed her as he fell blissfully into oblivion.

CHAPTER 27

"That was delicious!" Robert groaned as he finished his last bite of garlic bread. Erica had made an Italian feast of bowtie pasta mixed with tomatoes, broccoli, zucchini, smoked sausage and chicken in an alfredo sauce, served with garlic bread and salad.

"I'm glad you liked it," Erica said proudly. "Wait until you taste my homemade tiramisu. It's heaven in your mouth."

"I have no doubt that it's delicious, but I've had heaven in my mouth," Robert winked.

Erica laughed and tossed her napkin at her dinner companion.

"You are incorrigible! And because of that, you can do the dishes," Erica teased.

"I'd be happy to," Robert said. Being the only boy in a house full of girls made him no stranger to standing at the kitchen sink washing dishes after a delicious home-cooked meal.

"Don't be silly. I'd never make you clean up after me, especially since you worked all day," Erica said as she stood and began clearing the table.

Robert watched her for a moment. This was a far cry from the Erica he'd met this weekend.

"You're awfully domestic tonight," he mentioned.

Erica tossed her hair over her shoulder to glance at Robert.

"Two orgasms will do that to a girl," she winked and turned back to the sink and then challenged, "You should see what four will do."

Robert wrapped his arms around her from behind.

"Later. Right now, I'd love to talk about your day," he whispered.

Erica tensed. She knew it was coming. By the time she finally left her therapist's office, she hadn't had time to reduce the puffiness from her eyes and get dinner ready by the time Robert got home from work. *Home from work*. That sounded way too domestic, even in the mood she was in tonight!

"If you want," Erica agreed. "Do you want to talk over dessert?"

"Talk first. Then a shower. Then dessert in bed," Robert kissed her earlobe. "We may even get to the tiramisu."

Robert pulled Erica over to the couch where they had recently made love and stretched out with Erica curled into his chest. She fit so perfectly!

"So, why did you look like you'd been crying when I got here?" Robert asked, careful not to use the word *home*.

Erica said simply, "Because I had been, silly. Seriously, Pretty Boy, sometimes you have a knack for stating the obvious."

There's Erica! Robert thought to himself and chuckled.

"I mean," he tipped her chin up to look at him, "what or who *made* you cry?"

"Oh, that," Erica said lightly.

"Yes, that," Robert said. "Of course, if you want to talk about it."

Erica got very still and very quiet. She *did* want to talk about *some* of it.

"I had lunch with Brock today," Erica blurted out.

Robert tensed at the mention of Brock's name.

"I remembered you telling him that you would have lunch with him today. It actually bore a hole in my stomach all day, if I'm telling the truth," Robert confessed. "How did it go?"

"As well as could be expected, I guess," Erica shrugged. "He's been a really good friend to me over the past few months."

"It seemed more than that," Robert pointed out.

Erica thought for a moment and then said, "To him, maybe. He wanted more, but there was no connection for me other than the fact that I really like him. He's a great guy."

"I'll take your word for that," Robert said between clenched teeth.

Erica sat up and turned to look at Robert.

"You can't honestly be jealous? After what I showed you last night, what I told you…" Erica trailed off.

Robert needed to diffuse the conversation. They had been doing so well.

"Jealous? A little, maybe," Robert admitted, "But not insanely so. If he's truly your friend and respects your boundaries, he and I won't have a problem."

Erica relaxed a little.

"He knows where I stand. Brock knows that he and I will only ever be friends. He won't be coming back to the house," Erica said firmly. "Besides, he's still in love with his ex-wife, and I told him that he needed to go talk with her."

"The house?" Robert asked.

"Yes, the house. Boy, are the girls going to miss him!" Erica shook her head and laughed to herself thinking back at some of Brock's adventures.

"The girls?" Robert asked again.

Erica realized that she'd said too much and wasn't quite ready to go down this road with Robert. She had until Friday and wanted to make the most of their time together before then.

She patted Robert on the knee and said, "Friday, Pretty Boy."

"Friday, then," he agreed.

To change the subject, Erica offered, "Oh, I saw my therapist today. Your ears must have been bur-*ning*!" Erica punctuated the end with a light-hearted whistle.

"Really?" Robert's curiosity was piqued. "Do tell."

"Uh-uh. Patient-doctor confidentiality and all that," Erica teased.

Robert pulled Erica tighter.

"Come on! You can't tell a guy that he was the topic of conversation with your *therapist* and *not* tell him what you talked about!"

"My lips are sealed, Pretty Boy," Erica zipped her lips with her fingers.

Robert grinned devilishly.

"We'll see about that!" and began tickling Erica. He'd always gotten confessions from his sisters while they were growing up will a well-placed tickle. Besides, he loved to hear Erica laugh.

Erica squealed and squirmed trying to get away from Robert, but he was too big and too strong. When she realized that she was trapped under Robert and couldn't get away, the icy hand of panic grabbed her. She went from laughing to screaming and pushing while tears spilled from her eyes.

Robert stopped immediately and grabbed her carefully at the top of her arms.

"Hey, hey, Baby. Erica. It's me. Robert," he tried soothing her, anything to release the grip fear had on her. "It's okay. Shhh. It's okay. I promise. I'm so sorry."

Her eyes cleared, and she was back with Robert and not pinned on the football field under Kurt. Panic released her, and she collapsed against his chest.

"I'm sorry," she said, drying her tears.

"Don't you dare apologize to me. I'm the one who is sorry. I never meant to…" Unable to complete his apology because of the lump in his throat, he pulled her into him tighter. He couldn't find the right words to comfort Erica. The fear on her face was frightening, and knowing that he'd caused it made the delicious dinner he'd just eaten curdle in his stomach.

"I know. I know. I know," Erica shivered against him and wiped away the last of her tears. "You would never…"

Robert cut her off. "I would NEVER."

Erica shook her head that, again, she knew and curled back into Robert's arms. She shivered again, trying to shake off the feeling of panic.

"Let's get you into a warm bath," Robert offered.

"Will you get in with me," Erica's voice sounded as soft as a child and broke Robert's heart.

"You couldn't keep me out, Princess," he assured her. "Let's go. It's a bath, comfy pajamas and then dessert in bed for you."

Erica let Robert pull her up into his arms and into a sweet kiss. She knew he would never hurt her.

Robert was her safe place.

CHAPTER 28

Erica woke up Friday morning the same way she had woken up every morning since meeting Robert, wrapped in his strong arms. She squinted at the clock on the nightstand. There was still a little more than an hour before the blasted thing would go off, tearing Robert away from her. Those hours apart were the longest of her days. Oh, she wasn't sitting idly by waiting for his return by any means; she would never be *that* woman.

Erica had spent her days this past week doing what she'd always done. She'd kept her weekly Tuesday lunch with Daddy. He'd noticed a difference in her, a happiness, he'd said. He'd wanted to know all about it. All Erica had told him was that she'd met someone and that she'd been making progress with Dr. Boyd.

Daddy had been intrigued by the prospect of the "someone." In all of the years since high school, Erica had never mentioned a "someone" to her father. He'd wanted to meet the man who had broken through his daughter's defenses enough to be brought up in conversation. Erica placated him with her *all-in-due-time* offer. Randolph Spencer wasn't a man many people could say no to or put off to a later date, but to Erica he was simply "Daddy," and a kiss on the cheek and a smile from his Princess was all it took to bend him to her will.

She'd shopped all day Wednesday. She'd needed new lingerie for Robert. He deserved to see her in things other men hadn't. She'd also bought him a new couch for his apartment and had surprised him Wednesday night with its delivery. Instead of the muted blue, it was a bright, bold green, like the dress she'd worn Sunday. It had gone beautifully with his light-colored wood floors. She'd successfully exorcised the ghost from his bed, but the couch had remained a symbol of his torture and had needed to be replaced. She'd seen it in a showroom during her shopping trip and had bought it without a second thought.

Robert had balked a little Wednesday evening to her spending the money on the new couch, but, as with Daddy, he hadn't fought her long. A smile and a wink had been all it had taken for him to agree to

let it stay. The couch's fate was sealed when she'd dropped her dress

and draped her naked body over it to show how perfectly it went with

her skin and hair. They'd made love all evening in every position

possible on the new couch after Robert had agreed that it did, indeed,

go perfectly with Erica and that the two looked perfect in his

apartment.

On Thursday, she'd kept her standing appointment with Dr.

Boyd, and they'd delved deeper into her growing feelings about

Robert, her panicked reaction to being tickled by him Monday evening

and her dread about taking him to the house the next evening.

Erica had told Dr. Boyd about how wonderful Robert had

reacted Monday evening. He'd drawn a hot bubble bath for the two of

them and had washed her hair and massaged her body with her

expensive bath oil so that all of her panic, worry and tension went

down the drain with the water. He'd dried her hair patiently, put her

into comfy, flannel pajamas and found some silly sitcom marathon on

television. They'd cuddled on the couch watching TV and indulging in

the tiramisu she'd made for them before he'd whisked her away to bed

to simply wrap her in his arms. She'd gone to sleep that night with him humming the song they'd slow danced to last weekend in his

bedroom. Wrapped in his arms, she had truly felt that she was the joy

of his life. He certainly was hers.

Robert was breathing peacefully into her ear with his arms

wrapped tightly around her. It was the same position they'd slept in

each night, whether they'd made love or not. Her body molded

perfectly into his. She loved the sound of his gentle snoring and the

way his warm breath felt on her skin. She loved the way he would

reflexively hold her tighter if she shifted her weight in bed. She loved

the feel of his morning erection pressing into her bottom and the growl

he would give her if she wriggled against it. She loved everything

about the two of them together.

Yet she hated weekday mornings, and this one was worse.

Today was Friday. Today was the day. Today, she would take Robert

to her house and introduce one life to the other. She still wasn't sure

she wanted to do that. Though she wasn't ashamed of the life she'd

led, she was growing increasingly happy with the life she'd discovered

this past week in Robert's arms. She had been surprised that she

enjoyed the normalcy of dinner at home each evening, whether it was

her place or his. She had especially been surprised that she hadn't even thought about going to the club to find new partners or sharing Robert with anyone else. He was more than enough, and that thought made her smile and snuggle into his arms even deeper.

She dared one more glance at the clock, dreading the arrival of the morning rush to the door. The time was 7:05. She popped up, and strong arms pulled her back down. Robert was going to be late. He was always up by 6:45 and in the shower by 7:00.

"The alarm didn't go off! You're going to be late!" Erica sounded the alarm for him.

Robert groaned sleepily and pulled her closer.

"Get up, Sleepy Head," Erica wriggled against him.

Robert groaned again.

"If you haven't noticed, I'm already up," he said as he ground against her bottom.

Erica giggled.

"No time for that. You're going to be late."

"No, I'm not," Robert said between kisses to her shoulder.

"Yes, you are," Erica argued.

"I can't be late when I took the day off to spend it with you," he punctuated with a nibble to the back of her neck.

Erica flipped over.

"Why didn't you tell me?! I've been lying here dreading that damned alarm going off all morning when I could have been asleep!"

Robert swept flaming curls away from her flaming eyes of heated blue steel.

"There's this wonderful concept called 'surprise.' I thought I'd give it a try," he answered. "Wanna spend the day with me, Princess?"

The panic of him being late and the frustration of realizing that she'd robbed herself of an hour of sleep for no reason melted away with his invitation. It had been only four days since the last time she'd been able to spend an entire day with Robert, but it had seemed like forever.

"How could I resist?" she answered him back with a squeal of happiness and crashed against him.

Robert laughed and pulled her tightly into him.

"Now, can we please remedy the fact that I'm *up* so that we can go back to sleep?"

"My pleasure, Pretty Boy," Erica cooed as she climbed on top of her mount.

Robert sat up and wrapped his sleepy arms around the sexiest alarm clock he'd ever seen.

"If all snooze buttons felt like you, no one would ever get out of bed," he grinned.

Erica laughed as she set an easy rhythm, loving how natural and fun making love to Robert had become.

CHAPTER 29

Erica and Robert had spent all day in bed. They'd snacked on fruit, cheese and crackers to keep up their strength between sex and naps. Heaven couldn't have been any more perfect, Robert remembered thinking as he held his napping vixen in his arms.

He swept some of Erica's hair away from her shoulder and gently kissed the exposed porcelain skin underneath. Erica took in a deep breath and yawned.

"Hi, Sleeping Beauty," Robert kissed her skin again.

"Mmmmhmmm," Erica hummed.

"It's getting to be late afternoon, and I'm starving for some sustenance. Do you want to go out to dinner before heading out tonight?" Robert asked between kisses across her shoulder and up her neck.

"Shit," Erica groaned and looked at the clock. "I didn't realize how late it was getting."

She rolled over to look at Robert. Oh, he was so pretty!

"So…dinner?" he asked as his stomach growled.

"Sorry, I was distracted by how pretty you are," Erica teased and gave him a quick kiss. "Dinner. Hmm. Going out might not be a good idea."

Robert furrowed his brow.

"Why's that?" he asked.

"Well, there's a certain way I dress when I go to the house. It's what my guests expect, and it all plays a part in the atmosphere of the evening. If you're going to see everything, I owe you the full effect," Erica offered slowly.

"Oh," was all Robert could draw out of his vocabulary.

"So, it might not be appropriate to go out," Erica finished. "Still, if you want to call in an order for a couple of steaks, I could definitely go for some red meat before going out. I can get ready while you're picking it up. We can eat when you get back and then head out, if that's okay with you."

There was so much Robert wanted to know. There were questions he wanted to ask, but everything was trumped by the way the word *steak* made his stomach start gnawing on itself.

"Okay," Robert shrugged. "I'll grab a quick shower and call in an order for us."

The dread Erica had been feeling all week woke up inside her gut and started stomping around as she watched him crawl out of bed and head to the shower. That same dread stayed with her as she called and canceled her standing car service for the evening to take her to the house but kept her from canceling its return trip to pick her up Saturday afternoon to bring her back to the city.

Robert stood in Erica's shower and let the hot water wash over his muscles. Tension was creeping in as the evening got closer. He'd seen the change in Erica's eyes each time she'd mentioned the house this week. A huge part of him didn't even want to go tonight, didn't even want to know what the damned thing was, but he had to. He had to answer that gnawing part of him that chewed into his subconscious just like hunger gnawed at the lining of this stomach.

Whatever it was that needed to be seen, though, it couldn't be more than the way he felt about Erica. He had been happier in the past week than he'd ever been. She completed a part of him that he didn't even know he'd been missing. Their connection was intense but easy, and though he knew, intelligently, that there was no change in the physical makeup of his heart, it still felt bigger, fuller and beat with a steadier rhythm than it had before. It was as if she'd filled him with part of herself, and he would keep that part safe at all costs. After feeling what life was like with Erica, there was no way that he could go back to *before*, house of fantasy be damned.

Robert felt better after scrubbing everything harder than necessary. There was a greater conviction coursing through his body as he stepped out of the shower. There was greater devotion growing in his soul as he shaved his square jaw, and by the time he'd finished his grooming and stepped into the black slacks and red V-neck sweater he'd brought for the night, he felt that he was ready to face whatever Erica needed to show him. However, first he must take care of his growing need for food.

Robert walked into Erica's private bedroom, the one they'd shared together each night they'd spent at her place since she showed it to him Sunday evening. She was stretched naked across the bed nibbling on the last of the grapes looking like an ancient Greek goddess waiting to be worshiped.

"Well, you certainly make it difficult for a man to walk away," Robert remarked as he fastened his watch on his wrist.

"That's a good thing, right," Erica winked as she sucked the last grape into her mouth, grinning as Robert growled.

He sat on the bed to put on his socks and shoes, and Erica couldn't resist crawling over to him.

"I'm going to put you over me knee and spank you one day," Robert playfully threatened as she nibbled on his ear lobe.

"Promises, promises," she breathed into his ear.

"You'll see," he said as he stood quickly and gave her a quick slap across her, smiling wickedly at her surprised yelp. "But now, my goddess, we need food. I'll call on my way out and be back as quickly as I can."

Erica rubbed her bottom.

"Hurry back, Pretty Boy."

Robert bent and kissed Erica much more deeply than he had intended.

"Try to keep me away, Princess," he said breathlessly as he pulled himself away and turned to go while he still had the strength the walk out the door. The knowledge that he was returning as quickly as two steaks could be cooked was the only thing that made him able to leave her naked and wanting amidst the tangle of luxury pink sheets.

Erica watched him leave, longing for him to stay.

Had she known that it wasn't the only time she'd watch him walk away tonight, she would have begged him to stay, taken him back to bed and not let him leave it until work Monday morning.

CHAPTER 30

"Princess, I have returned with your red meat," Robert announced as he dropped the takeout bags on the kitchen table.

"Well, it's about time you return from your hunt," her smart mouth greeted him from the hall.

A smart-ass response died on Robert's tongue as he looked up to see Erica standing at the entrance to the kitchen. She stood there in black leather from head to toe. Stiletto, thigh-high leather boots and leggings covered her shapely legs. Her bodice was ensnared in a black leather corset with red leather laces up the front that tied into a deceptively innocent bow in between cleavage that threatened to spill over the top of the garment. A red and black amulet rested at the top of her mounds, drawing unnecessary attention to her gorgeous curves, though there was no way they could be ignored. Her fiery hair was pulled tightly back from her face into a ponytail that flared out in curly flames down her back. She wore heavier eye makeup that made the blue in her eyes more severe, and her glossy lips made him want to hear his name coming from them like a prayer as he made her come.

Erica stood there with her hands on her hips and tapped her toe waiting on Robert's appraisal.

"Well?" she spun around slowly.

Dammit, Robert thought to himself. The back was just as hot as the front. The leather leggings shaped her perfect ass even more perfectly, and the thick flames of her hair pointed the way to it. Suddenly, the steak was forgotten.

Erica cleared her throat as she finished her spin.

"I said, 'well,'" she demanded a response.

Robert nodded his appreciation.

"There are no words, Princess," he said, and clarified at the confusion that swept across her face, "And that is a very good thing."

Erica smiled, sauntered over to her hero and draped her arms around his neck.

"Good. Let's eat. I'm starved," she growled suggestively.

"Food? Now," Robert groaned.

"*You* were the one demanding food earlier. Now I'm hungry. Let's eat and then get going," Erica said firmly. She was certainly slipping into Mistress Erica.

"Fine," Robert gave in. "But, I am going to peel you out of all of this later."

"Damn right you are," Erica kissed him quickly and then turned to get some wine to go with dinner.

Robert set out the Styrofoam takeout plates, and Erica brought over wine and utensils. Both quietly devoured the steaks, grilled vegetables and roasted potatoes while draining their glasses of wine. Sated with food, Robert cleared the table while Erica excused herself to freshen up.

"Are you ready to go?" Erica asked as she came back into the kitchen.

"I'm ready to go so that I can get back here and bury myself in you," Robert said as he placed the last wine glass into the cabinet. He meant that, too. No matter what she showed him tonight, no matter what sexual fantasy or pleasure played out in front of him or beckoned for him, all he wanted was to come back here, take Erica back to her bedroom and show her that she was all that he ever needed.

"You say that now," Erica trailed off, her confidence shaken as she pictured Robert taking in the wonders that were about to reveal themselves to him.

He turned and leaned against the counter.

"Erica," he said heatedly. "No matter what, *you* will *always* be my fantasy. *You* will *always* be more than I could ever handle. It'll always be you. I hope you know that."

Erica lowered her head. Oh, how she hoped he meant that. She knew and had seen first-hand, many times in her house, how weak the flesh was. Hell, it was one of the things that she'd always loved. She loved the power that weak flesh gave her when she exerted her will over it. Now, she prayed to a deity she wasn't sure would listen to her that Robert's flesh would be strong. She desperately needed Robert's flesh to be strong tonight.

"Erica, please," Robert closed the space between them in a few long strides. "Tell me that you know that."

Erica looked up into his eyes and felt them burn through her.

"I won't lie to you, Pretty Boy. I'm nervous," she admitted. "All I know is that if we are going to move forward, I have to show you everything. I have to ease your curiosity. I have to show you what this part of me is, and I have to reconcile some things inside of my mind at the same time."

"Well, then," he offered his arm to her. "Let's go so that we can get this over with and get back here."

Erica linked her arm into his. "Yes, let's."

CHAPTER 31

The drive to the house had been quiet; both companions spent it in quiet contemplation. Erica spent the drive repeating Robert's passionate declaration that she would be enough. Robert spent the drive clearing his mind so that he could be open to Erica's revelation.

Nothing prepared him for what lay before him.

Sex was everywhere.

It was on the walls in the form of art. It was on tables and in corners in the form of statues. It was on the theater-size television that dominated the wall at the back of the room in the form of porn, but most of all, it was living and breathing in front of him.

He saw the perfect asses of two blondes as they bent over the cock of a very ecstatic man. He had a firm grip of their hair in both hands and took turns pulling one face up to kiss him while the other sucked him.

A busty brunette was bent over grabbing her ankles as another brunette pounded into her from behind while wearing a massive strap-on. Both women's breasts bounced hard and fast with the force of the penetration.

A beautiful man leaned against the far wall for support as another man knelt before him hollowing his cheeks as he sucked the receiver's tremendous length into his mouth. The other man's cock looked painfully hard as he stroked himself in rhythm to the sucking.

Everywhere Robert looked there was sex in different stages. Some were just beginning. Some were just building up, and cries of orgasms came from down the hall, behind him from the kitchen and from the man on the couch as he spewed over the full breasts of what he could tell now were twins.

Robert's cock grew hard as the twins rubbed the fluid into their breasts and giggled. Once finished, they stood and walked over to greet Erica.

"Hello, Mistress," one blonde bowed.

"Hello, Mistress," the other blonde followed.

Erica tensed on their approach. She was feeling exceptionally territorial as they neared her and Robert.

"Di. Sky. Thank you for coming," Erica played the perfect hostess.

The girls giggled.

"Are you going to introduce us?" Di asked, eyeing Robert.

Erica's voice dropped an octave.

"Robert, this is Di and her twin, Sky. Di and Sky, this is Robert," Erica made the introductions.

"Nice to meet you," Robert cleared his throat and nodded to the naked beauties in front of him.

The girls giggled again, and one of them – Robert couldn't tell them apart and had no blood flow going to his brain to try – explained, "It's really Dianna and Skylar, but…" one began while the other finished, "Di and Sky rhyme, and that's much more fun."

The one who was interrupted looked over at Erica.

"Will we get to play with him?" she asked eagerly.

Erica felt if she were to get any tenser that she would explode from her tight clothes.

"That remains to be seen," she answered through gritted teeth. "I have to finish showing Robert around. Go find another playmate for the time being."

"Yes, ma'am," they answered in unison and walked away.

Robert shook his head. *Did that really just happen?*

What followed was a tour through an erotic wonderland that led up the stairs to Erica's private quarters.

This room was more like the playroom in her apartment. There were chests of toys, displays of paddles, canes and chains. There was a suspension system along the ceiling and a Saint Andrews cross on the wall. A black leather mattress sat atop a platform in the middle of the room and restraints dangled from eight locations. This was a room built for sex.

This was the other side of Erica.

She walked across and sat on the edge of the bed. Curiosity, jealousy and anger battled for control of her emotions.

"Well, you haven't run away screaming yet," Erica broken the silence.

Robert stood there trying to reconcile the Princess in her pink and silver room to the woman sitting across from him.

"I don't know what to say," he said weakly.

"You've used that excuse already tonight when you saw me in

this," she swiped her hand down her body to indicate the clothes she was wearing. In this house tonight, it felt more like a uniform, what was expected. She felt like she was returning to work after a week of vacation where she had been someone else, living a life that wasn't meant for her. "Try again, Pretty Boy."

Robert was truly at a loss, but he knew they needed to talk. It was just difficult to do here, with her dressed like that, with the sounds from below echoing into the room.

"So, last Friday, you picked Ginger and me up in the club with the intention of making us part of *this*?" Robert sounded more disgusted than he'd meant. Nothing was going like it was supposed to go.

Erica felt like she'd been slapped.

"*This*?" Erica echoed back. "You didn't seem as disgusted with *this* downstairs when the girls were fucking you with their eyes."

This was going all wrong, but Robert couldn't correct it. He couldn't think clearly. He needed to get out of this house and back to neutral ground so that they could talk.

Erica mistook Robert's silence for agreement. "You want them?" Erica spat at him. "I'll go get them for you!"

Erica stormed past Robert, hurt burning its way through her insides as she moved toward the door. Tears threatened her eyes as she screamed down the stairs, "Di! Sky! Get up here!" Anger dammed her tears as she saw the beautiful, naked twins bounding up the stairs.

"Erica, don't. I don't want this. I want…" Robert was struck speechless as the girls entered the room and ran straight to him. Before he could move, one blonde was unbuckling his belt while the other had dropped to her knees to unzip his pants.

"So, I'm enough for you, huh?!" Erica spewed venom. "I'll always be enough?!"

Robert's eyes closed briefly as one of the girls put his exposed cock in her mouth.

"Dammit!" he screamed. "It's not supposed to be like this!"

Erica ran out of the room, tears streaming down her face as Robert pushed the girls away before they could go any further. He had to get to Erica!

"Erica! Erica, wait!" he followed behind her as the girls stood confused in the doorway.

His cock hurt from being denied. His head hurt from trying to concentrate. His heart hurt from watching Erica cry.

Erica reached the bottom of the stairs before he could and threw herself between two naked men on the couch. She popped her corset open and pulled both men to her exposed breasts.

"Erica, what are you doing?!?!" Anger ripped through Robert.

"If you can fuck two, so can I!" she screamed back. "And I'm so much better at it!"

"I don't – I want – I want you! Don't you know that?"

Erica closed her eyes as one of the men bit her hard.

Fuck! There was too much going on at once for Robert to think clearly. He ran from the bottom of the stairs and pulled Erica from the two men. She stood there in the center of the room, topless, mascara streaking her tear-stained face.

"Fuck you, Robert! You're weak, just like everyone else!" she spat at him.

They needed to get out of there. Now!

"Can we talk about this anywhere but here," he begged.

"No! Get out!"

"Erica, please," it worked the first night they were together.

Erica wasn't buying it this time.

She leveled her stare at Robert, dropped her voice low and

demanded, "Get out now."

"No. No. NO!" Robert screamed back.

The action in the house stilled. All eyes were on the spectacle as it unfolded.

"You wanted to FUCK them! I was supposed to be ENOUGH!" Erica shouted, the pain ripping through her evident as her voice shook.

"You can't blame my body for responding! You fucking brought them to me and dropped them at my feet. I don't want them! I want you!" Robert said quickly, anger and grief fighting for control. "It's always you. It will always be YOU!"

"GET OUT!" Erica's defenses were back up. He wasn't getting back in no matter how much he'd beg. The vision of the twins at his feet, the desire as he closed his eyes, was more than she could handle. She was destroyed on the inside, but she would rebuild. She'd done it before.

"Erica, please," Robert tried again, tears coming in full force now. "I…"

"You what?" Erica mocked.

Robert tried one last weapon, one last chance to break through the walls she'd built back so quickly.

"I love you," he answered simply.

Erica stumbled, but the pain coursing through her body was too intense. He had to go. He wasn't meant for her. She wasn't meant for him. He represented a fairytale, and fairytales did not exist. The life she'd chosen so long ago was familiar. It was all she knew. The vacation from that life was nice, but it was temporary, just like a vacation always was. It had to end.

She would end it before there was any more pain.

Erica did the only thing she knew to do to make Robert leave.

She turned her back on the life Robert represented and faced the only life she knew, the only one she was worthy of, and sat back on the couch to welcome back the two men who were worshiping her earlier.

They cautiously walked back to her and knelt before her.

With tears in her eyes, she looked at Robert while pulling the men's faces to her breasts.

"Go!" she demanded.

The two-letter word was a wrecking ball to Robert's core. If he didn't leave now, he was going to rip everyone in this room apart and tear the house down brick by brick. So, he did the only thing he could do to protect himself.

Robert turned his back and walked out of the house and away from the nightmare unfolding in front of him.

Erica watched the man of her dreams walk out on her for the last time. When she heard the door slam behind him, she shoved the men away from her body and tore up the stairs to the privacy of her room where she screamed until there was nothing left inside of her.

CHAPTER 32

I love you.

Go!

"NO!" Erica woke up from a nightmare and reached across the bed for Robert's familiar warmth. The only thing she found, though, was the cold leather that covered the mattress in her private room there at the house. She sat up and cringed as her bare skin made a disgusting ripping sound as it separated from the leather underneath. She'd apparently succumbed to sleep sometime between her screaming and crying. Looking around, she realized that she was alone.

Still topless from the night before, Erica stumbled in her stiletto boots to the closet and found a robe. She sat of the floor of the closet and stripped off her boots and then stood to peel herself out of her leather leggings.

I am going to peel you out of all this later.

Damn right you are!

Erica's body shook the chill that heartache always brings, and she shrugged into her robe. Determined to keep the threatening tears at bay, at least for the time being, she figured that she might as well see what mess the house was in after last night's event.

Erica stepped out of her room and called down the stairs.

"Hello?"

There were usually several lovers who imbibed too much and stayed the night, but the house seemed oddly still.

There was no answer.

Erica descended the stairs and looked around. No one was there. She checked the rooms one by one, and her suspicions were confirmed. There was no one. There were so many witnesses to her humiliation and heartbreak, but there was no one to cry to this morning. There were no friends to call to check on her. There were no call-me-later notes on the kitchen counter. She'd given Brock the kiss-off. Robert had left her.

In his defense, you made him go.

"SHUT UP!" Erica screamed back at the thoughts in her head.

The truth hurts.

Erica looked around again, and the enormity of the emptiness slammed into her. She was alone. She had no friends. She had no lover. All she had was money, a big empty sex house and a big empty apartment.

This time, the tears did come, and they hurt. They hurt as her body shook. They burned her dry, red eyes as they poured out from her shattered heart. They hurt as Robert's words bounced around inside of her splitting head.

No matter what, you will always be my fantasy. You will always be more than I could ever handle. It'll always be you.

I don't want them! I want you! It's always you. It will always be YOU!

Erica, please…

The last thing she heard before she stumbled, fell and descended into madness on the kitchen floor was his final declaration.

I love you.

Erica pulled her robe around her to get warm as she rocked back and forth in the middle of the cold linoleum.

I love you.

"I love you, too," she sobbed.

I love you.

"I LOVE YOU, TOO!" she screamed through another sob.

I love you.

"I LOVE YOU, TOOOOOOOOO!" ripped through her raw vocal cords.

I love you.

Erica had no voice left. From crying and screaming last night to the sobbing and screaming on the kitchen floor, she knew that she was done. There was no one to miss her. There was no one to come look for her.

Survival kicked in. She just needed to numb the pain, and then she could go on and be okay. God, everything hurt, and her brain screaming at her from inside was excruciating!

Numb the pain.

Numb the pain.

Her parties were drug free, but her salvation sat on the counter like a golden compass pointing the way to I-Don't-Give-A-Flying-Fuck-Ville. She pulled herself up and dragged her exhausted body to the counter. The neck of the tequila bottle felt foreign in her grip.

True, she was no stranger to the fiery demon, but she liked to keep her wits about her at parties and at the club. To drink was to let her guard down, to get sloppy.

Like with Robert.

"I told you to SHUT THE FUCK UP!" she screamed to no one before unscrewing the cap off the bottle and turning it up. She coughed as the fire she'd just swallowed burned its way through her worn body, and she thoughtlessly wiped her mouth with the sleeve of her robe.

Erica caught her reflection in the shiny toaster on the counter. She looked terrible! Mascara streaked her face, and her lipstick smeared across her chin. Her eyes were swollen and red, and her expertly coiffed ponytail was a shaggy mess.

She pointed to her reflection with the tequila bottle.

"You look like shit!" she scolded. "But never again. No one will hurt you and make you look like shit ever again!"

I love you.

She pointed to her reflection's head, and screamed, "I'm going to shut you up NOW!"

Erica turned up the tequila again and eased back to the floor. She sat there and drank until she threw up.

I love you.

She searched for more alcohol and drank until she passed out on the floor.

Erica drank each time she awoke and realized that her nightmares were real.

I love you.

Erica drank to quiet Robert's voice.

Erica drank to numb the pain in her chest where her broken heart was busy rebuilding its fortress.

For days, Erica sat in a heap on the kitchen floor, and she remained there – alone – until there was no more alcohol to be had. Robert's voice had now quieted to a low whisper that she could drown out more often than not.

Not knowing how much time had passed, Erica stood in the midst of her mess and allowed her sobriety to kick in. She had to get a shower and get clean. She had to find her phone. She had to *do* something; though what, she had no idea.

I love you.

"FUCK YOU," she screamed at his voice in her head as her heart secured the final bolt in her new, shiny steel-encased fortress and knew in that instant that she was going to be fine.

CHAPTER 33

Erica sat across from her therapist not saying a word.

"Do you want to tell me what happened, Erica?" Dr. Boyd tried to get Erica to speak.

Erica shook her head. The only reason she was sitting in the office now was because the good doctor had called Daddy and told him that she hadn't shown up to her sessions in over a month. After she'd canceled her weekly lunches with him and now the call from the doctor, Daddy had threatened to cut her off again if she didn't resume her sessions.

"You look more like a hung-over rock star than the woman I saw in my office a little over a month ago. I'll ask you again; what happened?" Dr. Boyd asserted.

Erica rolled her head from resting on her shoulder and leveled her eyes to her therapist's.

"What do you think happened?" Erica asked snidely.

"I think things at the house didn't go well for you and Robert," Delia answered bluntly.

Erica clapped her hands.

"Ding! Ding! Ding! Give the good doctor a prize!" Erica mocked her doctor.

Dr. Boyd simply stared. She knew that Erica was hurt. She also knew that spoiled brats lashed out when they were hurt and didn't get what they wanted. She had to proceed carefully, or she would lose Erica all together.

"*Why* didn't they go well? From what you were telling me, you and Robert were on the same page with your feelings for each other."

"Fine. You wanna know? They didn't go well because he was just like everyone else. He was weak. He wanted the twins. He wanted everything, and I gave it to him," Erica confessed.

Dr. Boyd quietly jotted some notes into her trusty legal pad and then looked up at Erica.

"And did he go through with 'everything'?" she asked simply.

Erica fell quiet again.

"Well, no, not exactly," she admitted.

Dr. Boyd scribbled more notes.

"I see. Then what *exactly* happened, Erica?"

Erica crossed her arms under her breasts and reluctantly relived that night and the next morning in horrid detail. She then confessed to drinking for most of the days and nights that followed and of having sex with strangers at the club, not being able to handle bringing them home. She'd also said how she'd blocked Robert's number from her phone so that she would not be tempted to pick up the phone when he'd called over and over again. Hearing his voice would have sent her running back to his arms, and she would not be weak again.

After Erica spilled everything that had happened since that fateful Friday, Dr. Boyd spoke.

"Erica, did you ever think that you purposefully ended the relationship to avoid any perceived chance of Robert ending it after your revelation?"

Dr. Boyd's question cut through the Patron hangover that had cursed Erica since waking at the ungodly hour of 9am to keep the appointment Daddy had set. Of course, she hadn't purposefully ended things! *Had she? FUCK! Not again!*

Dr. Boyd smiled. She knew she'd hit the nail on the head, and she saw the realization on Erica's face.

"When you were in here last," the therapist began carefully, "you confessed to being scared of so many things. You are a very strong woman. You've had to be, but with Robert, you felt that your feelings for him were a weakness. Do you think that your penchant for self-preservation read more into the evening than was really there, and you took it as an opportunity to get rid of your weakness?"

Erica fidgeted. She didn't want the doctor to be right *again*.

"You've totally self-destructed, Erica," Dr. Boyd continued. "Not only that, but from the looks of it, you've been on a downward spiral since that night. You don't look well."

Fuck that!

"Oh, you know you want me," Erica turned to her usual weapon. Sex trumped everything. Flesh was weak.

Dr. Boyd actually had the nerve to look offended, but Erica would not be swayed. She stood and began removing her blouse.

"Erica, I will only tell you once: Keep your clothes on," Dr. Boyd said firmly.

Erica narrowed her eyes. No one said no to her. *No one but*

Robert. FUCK!

"But you said I was beautiful," Erica said meekly. She wasn't used to rejection, and she didn't like it.

Dr. Boyd put down her pen and pad and walked over to Erica, but instead of kissing her like Erica anticipated, she redressed her, expertly putting her top back in place.

"You are beautiful, more so when you're not hung over, aggressive and angry," Dr. Boyd tried to explain away the hurt. "But I told you, you're one of millions to me. I love my wife. She is the only woman in this world to me, and she is the only one *for* me."

FUCK!

The realization that Dr. Boyd was right struck Erica so hard that it knocked her back onto the couch, but it wasn't enough to pull her out of the spiral she'd begun to rapidly descend. It wasn't enough to make her reach out to Robert, fall to her knees and ask him to come back to her. She was right that first morning when she'd though that he didn't deserve her concentrated crazy. She loved him too much to condemn such a good man to a life with her shattered pieces and messily-packed baggage. He would love again. Of this, she was certain. He was too good and too deserving not to.

But she, she would never love again. She would cherish the feeling of being loved, of being part of something bigger than her, but she would never know love again. Instead, she would pass the days with as many types of liquor as there were lovers. This was the life she knew. This was the life she deserved. She wasn't worthy of anything else.

"You look like you've made a decision, but I can't say it's for the best," Dr. Boyd observed with concern.

"It's the only one I can reconcile right now," Erica admitted and stopped her tears from escaping. She would not cry any more over the loss of love.

Dr. Boyd nodded in understanding.

"I have another patient in a few minutes, but promise me that you will keep your standing weekly appointment. We have a lot to work through, and I know we can do it. I know *you* can do it."

"I promise," Erica lied as she stood to go and walked out of the doctor's office for the last time.

CHAPTER 34

The first week without Erica had been torture. He'd called her over and over until her voicemail filled up and wouldn't accept any more messages. After that, he'd resorted to texting her but got no response. He'd driven to her apartment and knocked on the door. The doorman shook his head with pity the night Robert fell asleep on Erica's doorstep and left the next morning in the most chaste walk of shame in history wearing the same clothes from the night before.

He went to the club and watched at the bar for her.

The doorman took pity on him and gave him the number to her car service, but all they'd told him was that Miss Spencer didn't come to the door Saturday afternoon when they'd driven out to pick her up. They'd assumed she was *busy* and made other arrangements. The way they'd said *busy*, like they knew what went on in that house, made Robert's stomach churn.

In an act of final desperation after nearly a week of not hearing from her, he'd called her father. Randolph Spencer showed no concern for his daughter, saying that she was off being a Princess and when she was finished with her temper tantrum, she would be back. She did this every time she didn't get her way. Then he thanked Robert for calling and hung up on him without waiting for Robert's plea that someone needed to go out to that house and drag her out of it.

Someone.

He couldn't bring himself to drive back out *there*. Every time he closed his eyes, he could see the leeches hanging off of her breasts and her screaming at him to go. Fresh anger tore through him each time, and he knew that if he went out there and found her tangled up with *any* of them, he'd hurt someone – or worse. No, he couldn't go back *there*.

The first month without Erica was even worse than the first week. She still hadn't returned any of his messages. He just knew that she'd call his bluff in her spoiled-brat, smart-mouth way and call him after his last text.

THIS IS THE LAST ONE. IF I DON'T HEAR FROM YOU, I'LL KNOW IT'S OVER.

When she didn't call his bluff, reality had finally set in, and it had truly been his last text.

The color had gone out of his life. She'd taken it like a kid who takes her ball and goes to play in another sandbox when she didn't get her way.

The only color he had left was the green couch she'd bought him. It was so bright. It stuck out in the soft colors of his home like an emerald that caught the sunlight perfectly and blinded all who looked upon it. It radiated her boldness and her inability to blend in to her surroundings. Each time he walked past it, he remembered her draped across it like an Irish fantasy, naked with her red hair splayed out around her on its plush green cushions. From the dress and lingerie she'd worn the day she'd given him back his bed to the couch that now boldly stuck out in his apartment, he would always think of Erica when he saw green. Now, that splash of color was the only thing left of her.

That, and the hole she'd blown through his heart that nothing could fill. The beer that he drank every night after work at the same bar he'd once nursed the pain from Amelia's rejection, which he came to realize was a mere scratch compared to the destruction Erica left in her wake, did nothing to take up space. His mother's and sisters' hugs, jokes and phone calls to check on him only applied a little salve to the wound.

Nothing felt the same. Nothing tasted the same. Nothing *was* the same.

He'd known that Erica was The One. He'd known it from the first time he'd touched her. She'd both healed him and cursed him at the same time. One tiny little woman had turned his world upside down in the course of a week. One single week had changed everything.

After the second month without Erica, he'd finally stopped playing that fateful night over and over again in his head. He's stopped trying to analyze just where everything had broken down and went irrevocably wrong. He still didn't know, but at least he'd stopped obsessing over trying to find the *one thing* that would have made a difference.

The one thing he hadn't stopped doing was turning down advances from women at the bar. Sure, he was alone again, but none of them were Erica. None of them had her fire, and he desperately needed her warmth. None of them had her color or her flaming red hair or her bow-shaped lips that spouted the filthiest things when she came. None of them had her smart mouth that never ceased to make him laugh. None of them could ever bring the joy to his life that Erica had.

He went through each day mechanically. He did his job well. He functioned. He slept in the bed that Erica had exorcised so completely. He sat on the ostentatious green couch and watched silly sitcoms. He slipped into the comfortable bachelor routine that he was in before his dalliance with Amelia. Yet, he added two simple things to his routine: He checked his phone for Erica's call every night before he went to sleep and again every morning when he woke up.

Nothing.

Until now.

Robert sat on the same bar stool at the familiar bar absent-mindedly peeling the label from his beer bottle when his phone rang. He pulled it out of the pocket of his jeans and nearly dropped it.

ERICA CALLING.

He swallowed before answering.

"Hello? Erica?"

He wasn't prepared for what he heard next.

"Robert, please help me," she whispered into the phone before the line went dead.

CHAPTER 35

"Erica! ERICA!" Robert screamed into the phone like a madman.

Robert, please help me.

Robert called her back and only got her voicemail.

Robert dialed again.

Voicemail again.

"SHIT!" he yelled to no one.

The bartender came over to him.

"Robert, man, are you okay?" he asked with concern.

"No, Bobby. No I'm not," Robert shook his head and dialed Erica again while tossing enough cash on the bar to cover his tab for the night with a generous tip. "I've got to find someone."

Bobby grabbed the money and patted Robert on the shoulder.

"Good luck."

Robert thanked his faithful bartender and ran to his car. Once again, he tried Erica. Once again, there was no answer. He made a quick list of people he could call who might know where to find her, but it was a short list. On the short list, there was one name that he felt certain could help, but be damned if he wanted to call.

Robert, please help me.

Erica's plea trumped his pride as he looked up the number he needed. A cheerful voice asked him how she could direct his call. Robert took a deep breath before answering her.

"Detective Brock Samson, please."

"One moment," the cheerful voice replied.

Robert closed his eyes and pinched the bridge of his nose. It had only been a couple of minutes since Erica's call, but it had felt like forever, and he was still nowhere close to finding her or of knowing what kind of trouble she had gotten herself in to.

"Detective Samson," Brock answered.

Finally.

"Brock, it's Robert. I know I'm probably the last…" Robert began.

"What the hell do you want?" Brock interrupted.

"Have you seen Erica? Do you know where she is?" Robert tried to stay calm, but the worry in his voice betrayed him.

"What? No. I haven't seen her since our lunch a few months back. Why? What have you done?" Brock accused.

I left her, and now she's in trouble, Robert tortured himself.

"Look, she called me a few minutes ago and asked me to please help her, and then the line went dead. I tried calling her back several times, but it goes to her voicemail." Robert paused before adding, "She sounded scared."

"Shit!" Brock exploded. "I told her that she was going to get into trouble with the shit she does. Weren't you keeping an eye on her?"

Robert was kicked in the gut by his guilt.

"She ended things a couple of months ago. She won't return my calls. I haven't seen her or talked to her, which is how I know that something is really very wrong if she called *me*," Robert admitted. "Can you help me find her? Please!"

Robert hated how desperate he sounded, but he'd swallow his pride over and over again if it meant Erica was safe.

"I'll run a trace on her phone. If it's on, I should be able to locate her. You head toward the club and her apartment. Give me your cell number. I'll call you when I know something," Brock answered, and relief washed over Robert. Tears threatened to fall. Something was being done.

"Thanks, man," Robert choked out before rattling off his number.

"We'll find her," Brock's confidence as he ended the call helped Robert keep the panic at bay.

There was a plan.

He and Brock would find Erica, and she would be okay. He would keep her safe, and no amount of her telling him to go would make him leave her ever again. Of that he was certain.

Robert started his car, and the familiar rumble of the Camaro's engine heralded that the cavalry was on its way.

Erica would be okay.

She had to be.

CHAPTER 36

Erica found herself surrounded by three college-age jocks, football players from the looks of them, in a dark parking garage not far from her club. They'd managed to steer her drunken self into the trap after leaving the club for the night. After months of a downward spiral spent drinking painful memories away, sobriety and adrenaline quickly found its way through her bloodstream. She'd gotten in a quick call to Robert before the jerk who seemed to be the leader had snatched her phone from her. Robert was the first person who popped into her mind, which she found incredibly ironic since she'd taken up drinking to try to forget him.

"So, you finally notice us," the leader teased as the boys circled Erica like vultures.

Erica shook her head in confusion.

"Noticed you? What are you talking about?" she questioned in an effort to keep them talking. Robert would find her. She knew he would. She just needed to give him time.

"Every weekend we go to that club, and every weekend we watch you pick out people and then leave with them or take them somewhere in the back. Yet, you've never noticed us. We've got what you need, baby," he said and grabbed his crotch to the cheers of his friends.

Shit!

Erica looked from boy to boy in an effort to find a weak link. The other two never met her eyes, but they were showing no sign of helping her.

"Oh, is *that* what this is about?" Erica needed to keep him talking. "That's nothing, really. Just old friends…"

SMACK!

The pack leader slapped her into silence.

"Shut up, whore! I've seen the way you walk, the way to touch people, the way you dress. I've *watched* you."

Erica rubbed the sting from her cheek and said a silent prayer for Robert to please hurry.

"Look, if that's what you want, then I'm sure we can work

something out," she tried bargaining with her assailant.

He looked to his companions for support, and they nodded their heads. They all knew what they were going to do the moment they'd agreed to follow Erica out of the club. Had she been sober and thinking clearly, she would have agreed to Andre-the-Bouncer's offer to walk her home tonight. But no; in her infinite drunken wisdom, she said that she'd be fine. He'd given up when a fight broke out at the bar.

She was *so* not fine.

As they closed the circle tighter around her, Erica could smell the alcohol coming off of them, and it sickened her. Suddenly, she was back on the football field long ago with Kurt, and she knew what was about to happen. She was so small, and they were so big. Not only were they big, but there were also three of them! How was she supposed to fend off *three* of them?

Then it hit her as the two support guys grabbed her arms to restrain her.

She'd been wrong all these years. There wasn't safety in numbers. More people just meant that there was more pain to be had, and she knew with every alarm going off inside her head that this was going to hurt.

Erica turned her eyes upward and prayed again for Robert, this time out loud.

"You're begging for another man? Listen boys. She's *begging* for it." He grabbed her by her chin and made her look into his eyes. "I'm going to make you beg for *me*!"

The following backhand across her jaw brought the tears that she'd been successful at hiding since she first realized that she was in trouble. Just like that morning after at the house, there was no one to save her. There was no one to protect her. She was alone with three ravenous, drunken, massive football players intent on one thing: *Her.*

The aggressor ripped her dress down the front and pulled down the cups of her bra while his friends held her tight as she struggled.

"Look how they jiggle when you try to get away!" he slurred and grabbed at her.

Erica vomited at his touch.

He hit her again.

"You BITCH!"

He ripped her panties at the side and motioned for his boys to lay her on the hood of the minivan behind them.

"Hold her the fuck down," he demanded as he pulled a condom packet out of his jacket pocket and tore it with his teeth. He positioned his vomit-covered body between Erica's legs. "With as many people as you've fucked, a guy can't be too careful," he insulted before he slammed into her.

Erica felt ripped in two as he slammed into her again and again. She cried, but she would not beg. Instead, she closed her eyes and went to her safe place.

Robert was her safe place.

She was in his strong arms, and he was slowly spinning her around the room to their song. He sang softly in her ears about her being the joy of his life, and she knew that every word was true. His touch was gentle at the base of her back as he held her close, always careful not to hurt her. Then he whispered, "I love you, Erica."

As her safe-place Robert began her name, a booming voice finished it.

"ERICA!" screamed a familiar voice, but it was wrong. It wasn't Robert.

Erica opened her eyes.

BROCK! Oh, thank God! BROCK!

The boys scattered like cockroaches at the sound of Brock's voice and left Erica lying in a mess of tattered clothing, vomit and blood on top of the unoffending minivan.

Brock ran to her as she struggled to sit.

"Stay still, Erica," he ordered as he took off his jacket and covered her nakedness with it, careful not to destroy any evidence he could find. "We've got to get you to the hospital."

Erica panicked.

"NO! NO HOSPITAL! BROCK, PLEASE NO HOSPITAL!" she clung to his coat and begged. She would hurt, but she would heal. She couldn't go to the hospital. If word got out that she was attacked, it would be on the news, and her father would be so embarrassed. She didn't want that after all he'd done for her. On top of that, she'd been drinking *a lot* tonight. No one would believe her if she cried *rape* with a blood alcohol level as high as she was sure hers was. Besides, she'd been violated once tonight. She didn't want to be violated again.

"Erica, damn it! For once, can you please do what you're told?" Brock begged.

Erica moved and winced at the pain that ripped through her again. So much hurt.

"Brock, please. No hospital," she started crying again.

"Fine, but you have to see a doctor, Erica."

Doctor? Her mind flipped through an imaginary rolodex. Yes, a doctor!

"Please call Dr. Delia Boyd. Tell her what happened, and then ask her to bring her partner to my apartment," she offered. "She's my therapist, and her partner is an MD," she explained in an effort to clear Brock's confusion.

It was a good compromise. She would get to see a therapist and a medical doctor and make Brock feel better all at the same time.

Brock, like all of the men who loved her, could never deny Erica anything she'd wanted.

"Fine. I'll make the calls from the car. Let's get you out of here."

Once in the safety of Brock's unmarked car, Erica asked, "How did you know where to find me?"

Brock looked over at her before answering.

"Robert called me. He wasn't able to reach you after you called him asking for help. I traced your cellphone, and it led me to the parking garage. The guy is worried sick. I need to call him."

Erica's stomach rolled for the second time that evening. She didn't want Robert to see her like this.

"Not yet. Please," she asked her friend through her falling tears.

"Erica, he's going to be worried sick until he hears from me. I told him I would call him as soon as I found you and made sure you were okay. He swallowed his pride and asked for my help. The least I can do is swallow mine and call him back."

Not yet. Please not yet.

"Okay, so…you found me, but you haven't made sure that I'm okay yet." She loved the way her mind worked and marveled at the fact that it was working at all after what she'd been though tonight. "You can call him *after* I've seen the doctor. Okay?"

Brock ground his teeth in worry and frustration.

"Okay. First the doctor," Brock agreed.

Once moving, he'd made two phone calls. One was to Dr. Boyd as Erica had requested. She and her partner were on their way to Erica's apartment.

The other was to another detective for a favor. He needed evidence collected at the scene of an attack but needed it to stay quiet for now. Brock was known for doing things by the book and had earned the respect of many on the force. His request wasn't questioned, and crime scene technicians were on their way.

Erica glared at him as he ended the second call.

"Don't look at me like that. I compromised on the hospital. I will not compromise on the evidence. I will just keep your name out of it as long as I can," he said as he parked the car outside of her apartment building after the short drive. "Come on, let's get you upstairs and wait on the doctors."

CHAPTER 37

Robert paced the hallway outside of Erica's apartment. It took him what felt like an eternity to get there after he'd gotten Brock's phone call.

"Robert, I found her," Brock's voice was flat, procedural on the other end of the call.

"Is she okay? Where is she? I have to see her," Robert fired at once.

"She will *be okay, but before I tell you where she is, I have to tell you what happened so that you're prepared."*

Nothing could have prepared Robert for the things he heard Brock say, and now he was here waiting, going out of his mind to see her and to hold her. He had to wait, Brock had told him. There was a doctor in with her now doing an exam, and her therapist was in there, too. Brock was in the room, as a detective, making sure the sexual assault kit wasn't compromised. Erica told Brock that she didn't want to file charges, but Brock had insisted on the collection of evidence just in case she changed her mind after the shock had worn off.

Robert was full of so many emotions while waiting to go to her side. He was so angry at the monsters that hurt Erica. He felt guilt that he didn't try harder to make her listen to him; had he been able to make her understand, she wouldn't have been at the club alone tonight, and none of this would have happened. He felt horrified that she had to live this nightmare twice in her life. But most of all, he just felt the need to wrap her tiny body in his arms and protect her from the world.

Robert got to the end of the hall and turned to pace when Brock opened the door.

"You can come in now," he said, "but know that she took quite a beating tonight."

Robert nodded his head and walked toward the door.

His heart leapt into his throat when he saw her.

Erica was curled up in the fetal position on her leather couch underneath a pink plush blanket. She was wearing her plush robe that hung on the back of the door in her playroom. Her hair was matted in knots of dried fluids. She looked so much smaller than usual, but what struck him hardest were her eyes when she looked up at him. They looked so deep and sad and lost.

"Hi," she croaked, and the weakness in her voice broke him. He ran to her side.

"Hi," he replied through tears.

Erica reached up and wiped one of the tears from his cheek.

"I know, I look awful," she tried to joke.

Robert cautiously reached up and touched her face, carefully tracing her bruised jaw. Erica winced as he neared the corner of her busted, swollen lip, and he jerked his hand away. She quickly pulled it back and nuzzled his palm with her cheek.

"Please don't. You feel so warm," she said with such emotion.

Someone cleared a throat behind him, and he turned to look.

"Hi, Robert. I'm Dr. Stephanie Chambers," a tall, attractive woman introduced herself.

Not removing his hand from Erica's cheek, he turned his head to address the doctor.

"Thank you for coming, Dr. Chambers," he said politely.

"How is she?"

The doctor smiled warmly.

"She's strong. She's a fighter. She's going to be sore for a while, but she will heal," the doctor assured him. "I called in a prescription for some pain relievers and something to help her sleep. I gave her a dose of each to get her through tonight, and the pharmacy will deliver in the morning. I'd like to see her in a week just to recheck things, but she'll make a full physical recovery."

"And that's my cue," the other attractive woman, though more plain than her counterpart, said. "I'm Dr. Delia Boyd, Erica's therapist. Erica, when you feel up to moving around, come see me, and we can talk. But, if you need me sooner, call the number I gave you. It's my personal cell. I'll be right here."

Erica nodded weakly.

Robert said, "I'll see to it, Dr. Boyd. Again, thank you for coming and taking care of Erica tonight."

"We wouldn't have been anywhere else," Dr. Boyd assured him. "Take care of her. We're going to take off now and let her rest."

"Thank you, both, so much," Erica said as the doctors took their leave.

Erica and Robert watched as Dr. Chambers gave the sexual assault kit and a bag filled with Erica's torn clothing to Brock as she neared the door and the two exchanged cards. Once the doctors were gone, Brock announced that he, too, was leaving so that Erica could rest.

"The evidence has been collected. It's okay for you to take a warm bath, if you're not too tired," Brock told Erica.

Again, Erica nodded.

"Hey, I never thanked you for coming to my rescue tonight," she said through fresh tears.

"No thanks necessary, but I couldn't have known you needed rescuing without Robert. He was the one who called me," Brock said.

Robert stood and held out his hand. This time, Brock shook it.

"Thank you for everything. I don't know what I would have done…" Robert couldn't finish.

"Don't even think it. She's safe now," Brock said. "Just take care of her."

"There's nothing else that I want more," Robert assured the detective.

Brock bent to kiss Erica on her forehead.

"I'm headed out. I'll call tomorrow and check on you, okay?"

Erica replied, "I'd be hurt if you didn't."

Brock shook Robert's hand once more on his way out.

The sudden silence stretched between the former lovers and echoed through the apartment. It had been months since Robert had been here. So much had happened. There was so much that needed to be said, but for right now, in this moment, he just needed to take care of Erica, and she needed him to take care of her.

"So…what now?" Erica broke the silence.

Robert knelt down beside her once again and cupped her cheek.

"Now, you get a warm bath," he said.

Erica closed her eyes and took a deep breath.

"Will you come with me?" she asked softly.

"Try and stop me, Princess" he smiled at her and scooped her injured, battered body up in his arms and carried her to her bath.

CHAPTER 38

Erica leaned against Robert for support as he untied her robe and let it fall to the floor. The steam from the hot bath wrapped around her and felt so good. She couldn't wait to sink into the bath.

Fresh anger and tears flooded through Robert as he saw the bruises on her arms, wrists and legs. She had such perfect, porcelain skin that any mark to it was an injustice, much less marks caused by such despicable violence. He traced the outline of one of the offending marks on her wrist.

"Erica," he began.

Erica stopped him.

"Don't, please. Can we not talk right now?"

Although he wanted to declare his love, proclaim that he would find and punish the men who did this to her and promise that she would never be in danger again, more than anything, he wanted to give her what she wanted and be what she needed.

Robert nodded.

Erica smiled weakly.

"Thank you." She indicated the water, "Will you help me in?"

Robert scooped her up once again and lowered her into the luxury bathtub and watched as her battered body disappeared under the steaming water.

Erica's body hurt. Everything about it hurt, but when the hot water lapped at her core, she wanted to scream. Instead, she ground her teeth. Robert was torturing himself already, and she didn't want to add to it.

Through the nightmare tonight, one thing had been constant in her mind: Robert. He was the first person she'd thought to call. He was the safe place that protected her mind through the assault. His was the only touch she didn't feel she'd recoil from at the moment. Seeing him kneeling by the bathtub with such love and concern in his eyes, she was sure of one thing: She needed him. She couldn't get through this without him.

"Are you going to get in with me?" Erica asked.

Robert was shocked by her request.

The look on his face stung Erica more than the hot water had stung her fresh wounds.

"I'm sorry. I just thought…" she couldn't finish for the tears clogging her throat.

Robert was horrified that she misunderstood, and he had to make her understand his hesitation.

"Oh my God, Erica. Please don't cry. There is nothing I would love more than to climb into this bathtub and hold you and kiss you and try to take away your pain," he hoped she believed him because it was gospel. "It's just that, with what you've just been through, I didn't want to push you or rush you or…do anything to cause you to equate my touch to theirs."

Erica could never equate Robert's touch with the ones who had hurt her tonight, or to anyone. His touch was tender, even when rough. She'd trusted him from the very moment they'd met and may have loved him even then.

"Robert," Erica's voice cracked with emotion. "Please get in and hold me. I *need* you to hold me. Please?"

Robert could never deny her, so he slowly stepped out of his clothes and into the bathtub behind her. Wrapping her in his arms was like finding his home after being lost for so long. He wanted to pull her as tight to his body as she could stand, but she was hurt and sore. He had to be gentle.

"How's this?" he asked.

Erica sighed and melted into his chest.

"It's perfect. Thank you," she whispered.

Robert reluctantly let go of Erica long enough to help her lay down in the water to wet her hair. He used his hands to help saturate every strand and then guided her back to sitting. He lovingly lathered her mane with the fragrant shampoo that reminded him of autumn and made sure that every bit of vomit, blood, dirt and grime were washed out. Then he drained the tub to wash away all of the bad and refilled it with fresh, clean water. Robert carefully guided her back down to rinse. She looked like the fantastical mermaid from sailors' tales with her body submerged in the water and her red locks flowing around her. He repeated the process with the conditioner, and when he was done with her hair, he would wash her body, if she would allow it.

Erica loved the way he touched her, like she was so precious. No one had ever made her feel so valued and treasured. His hands felt so good in her hair as he cleaned it, and they felt even better supporting her body as he helped her lower into the water. There was gentleness in his strength, a male tenderness that touched her heart. She loved this man, and she would let him know that.

"Erica?" Robert interrupted her thought.

"Hmmm?" she asked as his voice cut through her silent reverie.

"May I?" he asked and nodded at the lathered cloth in his hand.

Erica nodded her permission.

"Are you sure?" Robert needed to know that she was okay with him touching her exposed body after such a traumatic event.

Erica smiled at him. He was even more handsome than her mind had remembered. He was her Pretty Boy.

"Pretty Boy, there's nothing I want more." Then she was serious. "Please, wash away their touch. Please. I need you to wash away their touch and replace it with yours."

Fresh tears filled Robert's eyes as he began at her neck and gently worked his way down, stopping to refresh the soap when it was needed. He washed and rinsed every inch of her battered body, wishing that he could wash away the memories of tonight just as easily as he'd washed away the grime.

Erica kept her eyes closed the entire time Robert spent washing her body. She was committing every stroke to memory, though there were no words in her vocabulary to describe how safe she felt in his arms.

Erica had turned to face Robert during the process and sat with her legs crossed in the tub. He rinsed the cloth free of soap, wrung the excess water out of it and gently wiped her face. Not only was he her safe place, but he also cared for her. It was a care that went deeper than physical love and was more powerful than lust.

"Do you want to know what helped me survive tonight?" Erica asked to break the silence.

Both afraid and curious, Robert encouraged her to tell him.

"I went to my safe place," Erica touched Robert's cheek and made him look her in the eye. "*You* are my safe place. When I realized what was going to happen and no one was there to stop it, I did the only thing I knew to do to protect myself from breaking. I thought about that night in your room when we danced, and you sang to me softly. That kept me strong. I wouldn't beg them to stop because they wouldn't have. Ravenous animals don't comprehend things like that, but I could protect my mind from snapping. I did that by thinking of you."

Robert searched her eyes and felt the passion in her words.

"If only I could have found you sooner…" he lowered his head, and she pulled it back up.

"But you were there; don't you see?" she assured him. "You protected me and kept me as safe as you could until Brock got there to stop it."

"But *I* didn't stop it," the guilt of not being the one to find her was eating him from the inside.

"Stop it. You did! You called Brock knowing that he could find me, and then you kept me safe *up here*," Erica pointed to her head. "Do you know what a wicked place my mind is? Was? I'm not sure anymore, but I did realize one thing."

"What was that?" Robert was curious.

"I had it all wrong all these years. There was never safety in numbers. That was proven tonight," Erica admitted.

Robert clenched his teeth.

"I still can't believe there were *three* of them!"

"Shhh … please. I can't think about that right now. Besides,

I'm baring my soul, if you hadn't noticed, Pretty Boy."

Robert loved her smart mouth. Even though it was cracked and swollen, it was still the most beautiful smart mouth he'd ever seen.

"Yes, ma'am," he grinned. "Please, tell me more."

"That's better. Thank you," she grinned back and melted his heart completely. "As I was saying, *you* are my safe place. You have been from our first night together. I knew it the moment you picked me up on your shoulders and laid me down on the bed. I was so free in that moment because there wasn't a moment of fear. Then, we when we made love that first time, and every time after, you never rushed in. I never flinched with you. Since Kurt, I flinched with everyone, even though the physical pain was long gone, but never with you. You've always been my safe place, and tonight, I realized that more than ever."

Robert tried to process her realization.

Before he could speak, she finished, "I think I loved you even then."

Robert blinked.

"What?" he asked, making sure he'd heard what he thought he'd heard.

Erica shook her head. Maybe telling him that was too much. Maybe he wasn't ready to hear it. Maybe he'd moved on in the time they'd spent apart. Maybe he was here tonight out of pity or obligation. She didn't want to say it again. She'd already been humiliated enough tonight.

"Please, say that again," Robert begged her. "I just need to make sure that I wasn't imagining those words coming from you. Please, Erica. Please tell me again."

The light in his eyes and the excitement in his voice encouraged Erica to tell him again.

"I said, 'I think I loved you even then,'" she admitted.

Robert smiled the smile she'd missed for so long. He smiled the genuine smile that touched his eyes and broke down even the newly built steel fortress around her heart.

"You loved me?" he asked and then looked away. "Past tense?"

This time she took his handsome face in both of her tiny hands, bruises and all, and looked into his misting eyes.

"I *love* you," she declared. "Past, present, future. I. Love. You. I love you. I love you," and then once more with feeling, "I love you,

Robert Cunningham."

Robert couldn't find his voice. He'd dreamed of her saying this, had been tormented in his sleep many, many nights over the past few months by her saying those words to him.

"Well, don't just sit there, Pretty Boy. Please say *something*."

Robert blurted out the first thing in his heart, and it felt so perfect.

"Marry me, Princess."

It was Erica's turn to be without words.

"Hmm? What?"

With conviction, Robert repeated, "I said, 'Marry me, Princess.'"

Erica was still in disbelief.

"I expected a heartfelt 'I love you, too,' but 'marry me?'" She was stunned.

Robert cautiously pulled her closer and rested his forehead against hers.

"I love you, Erica Spencer. I promise to love you, honor you and protect you for the rest of my life. Marry me. Please, Erica. Marry me," he breathed.

Suddenly the horror from the night's events faded. It was replaced with hope and happiness and love, love for this man and the hope and happiness she had for their future.

"Okay," she whispered.

Robert's smile got brighter.

"Okay? Are you sure?" he asked hopefully.

"Let's get married, Pretty Boy," Erica smiled back.

CHAPTER 39

Robert sat across from Randolph Spencer. The man's office looked as if it were designed with him as the centerpiece. Everything screamed money and power, from the leather winged back chairs to the Persian rug in the center of the room.

"So, *Robert* was it?" Spencer asked.

"Yes, sir."

"What can I do for you, Robert?"

Erica had no idea Robert had set up this meeting with her father after she'd agreed to marry him. She'd probably roll her eyes and say something smart, but he also knew how much she loved her father. He didn't need to ask his permission for her hand; she'd already given it happily. He was there hoping to get the man's blessing.

"Well, Mr. Spencer, I'm going to marry your daughter, and I was hoping you would give us your blessing," Robert said confidently, knowing that a man as busy as Randolph Spencer would appreciate the direct approach.

Spencer laughed. The laugh grew into a loud, booming, boisterous sound that filled the room. Robert let him laugh and waited for it to fade.

When he was finished, Spencer asked, "You mean my daughter, Erica? Petite, independent, smart-mouthed?"

Robert smiled. The man truly did know his daughter, though she'd kept the recent news of her assault from him. She didn't want to break his heart, she'd said.

"Yes, sir. You forgot fiery red hair, brilliant, Princess Erica," Robert fired back.

Spencer laughed again.

"So you *do* mean Erica."

"I do, indeed, sir."

Spencer's expression turned stern. Robert imagined that this look made an appearance at many a board meeting.

"I needed the laugh, son. Thank you, but let me ask you this," Spencer crossed his arms and leaned across his desk. "Why would I give you my blessing to marry my daughter?"

Robert was not intimidated by the man. In fact, he respected him.

"Because I love her, Mr. Spencer. What's more, she has found me worthy enough to love me in return." Robert hoped the man felt the sincerity in his declaration, but again, he didn't need permission, just his blessing. "I asked her to marry me, and she agreed. I'm here to get your blessing. She's told me how much she loves you, and I know it would mean the world to her."

The man studied Robert with his keen eyes, but Robert was unmoved.

"You've already asked her?" Spencer asked.

"Yes, sir."

"And she said yes?" he asked again.

"Yes, sir."

Spencer leaned back in his chair behind his large desk and shrugged his shoulders.

"Then who am I to stand in the way? I've never been able to deny my Princess anything she's ever wanted. If she loves you and has agreed to marry you, even if I didn't give my blessing to you right now, all she would do is kiss me on the cheek with a 'Please, Daddy,' and I'd give it to her then," the businessman confessed his weakness to Robert.

Robert nodded and laughed.

"She has the same power over me, sir," he also confessed.

"Then, you are worthy of her. Don't break her heart. Be good to her. She's seen a lot of hurt and disappointment in her life," his eyes darkened with an unspoken threat.

You don't know the half of it, Robert thought to himself.

"Mr. Spencer, I will always love her, lay down my life to protect her and work every single moment of my life to make her happy and to make her dreams come true."

Spencer took a deep breath and nodded.

"Thank you for coming to talk with me. I respect what you've done here, seeing as how you're getting married, whether or not I give my blessing."

Robert damned sure was.

"Sir, nothing could stop me from spending the rest of my life with Erica," Robert said, leaving no doubt.

Randolph Spencer stood and walked around his desk to stand

in front of Robert.

"Then, I give you my blessing to marry my Princess," he held out his hand to seal the deal.

Robert stood triumphant and shook his future father-in-law's hand.

"Thank you, sir."

CHAPTER 40

Erica sat at the vanity in their luxury hotel suite unpinning her hair thinking back on her wedding day.

Everything had been perfect. It was better than any fairytale she dreamed up when she was a girl. Robert had been her real-life Prince Charming waiting for her at the end of the aisle. Her mother had even made it in for the wedding and had been cordial to her father.

Her father. Robert had surprised her by getting his blessing. Most people were intimidated by Randolph Spencer, but not Robert. He walked right into his office, asked for his blessing and got it. Her father had lunch with Erica the next day and asked all about the man she was going to marry, and Erica gushed about how much she loved him and knew how much he loved her and how happy they were going to be. He had been happy to hear that Erica had sold her house in the country and was still seeing, and making great strides with, Dr. Boyd. He had been even happier to see his baby girl genuinely happy.

He'd cried when he saw her in her wedding gown in the choir room that had been converted to her dressing room at Robert's small country church. He'd cried walking her down the aisle but smiled the biggest smile she'd ever seen from him when he'd placed her hands in Robert's.

It was a smaller wedding that she'd fantasized about as a child, but it was the perfect size for the woman she'd matured to be. Robert's mother wiped away tears of happiness while his sisters grinned from ear to ear. Her mother sat politely beside her father and cried quiet, crocodile tears as dramatically as she could.

Even Brock was there, and apparently had followed her advice about reaching out to his ex-wife. She fit the description Brock gave her one night over a drunken confession of love and regret. Yet, there they sat, together. Erica smiled at him as she walked down the aisle. If she could find true love, then surely they could find their way back to each other.

Drs. Stephanie and Delia sat next to Brock and his ex-wife. The two doctors had saved her life as surely as Brock and Robert had.

She had been so happy that they'd come to witness the day they'd help create.

Though what had made her happiest that afternoon had been her groom. Every woman deserved to be looked at the way he looked at her when she appeared at the end of the aisle with her father. The happiness and pride he felt permeated his aura and was felt by everyone present. She felt his love for her when he accepted her hand from her father, and each word of his vows was undeniably filled with truth and love.

When he raised her veil to kiss his bride, Erica had held her breath for a moment. Then it hit her. This was real! This wasn't a fantasy she'd dreamed up. She was living every fantasy she'd ever had about finding love, from the devoted Prince to the massive, ostentatious wedding gown. All she had to do now was kiss her husband and live happily-ever-after.

And she did, much to the amusement of everyone in attendance. She'd lunged at him, wrapped her arms around his neck and kissed him passionately. He picked her up and swung her around. She was his, and he was hers!

After a beautiful, small reception and dancing all evening, they were finally alone. She stood examining her handiwork.

She wore a white silk, floor-length gown and accessorized it with her wedding pearls that Robert had left for her in her dressing room. Her hair was down, just the way her husband loved it.

"Wow," Robert whispered and clutched at his bare chest. "I am the luckiest man alive, Mrs. Cunningham."

Erica winked, "Yes, you are, Mr. Cunningham. And, might I add, you don't look so bad yourself in those silk boxers I bought you. Hot!" She fanned herself in appreciation.

Robert threw back his head and laughed.

"You truly are a beautiful sight," he professed.

Erica spun slowly so that he could get the full effect.

"Well, a girl only makes love to her *husband* for the first time once in her life. I wanted to look the part," she admitted.

Robert closed the distance between them and took her in his arms.

"Say it again," he breathed.

Erica giggled.

"My husband."

Robert groaned.

"Again."

"My husband," Erica repeated.

Robert crushed his lips to hers.

"My husband. My husband. My husband," she made out through his kisses.

Robert scooped up his bride and carried her to bed.

Erica looked up at her husband from underneath him.

"I'm going to love you forever, you know," she admitted.

Robert smiled down at her.

"I'm going to love you forever, too, you know," he mirrored back.

Erica nodded and pulled his lips to hers. She needed to be with her husband, to feel him inside of her. Her body ached for his touch. Her emptiness needed to be filled. She pulled his body closer to hers as greedily as she could.

Robert growled against her skin and sent shockwaves to her core.

"You're really going to have to take me now," she pulled his face away from her neck long enough to give him the order.

He laughed.

"What, no sweet, slow wedding-night first time?" he teased, knowing good and well that he needed her as much as she needed him.

"After waiting a month?!?!" Erica exclaimed in mock exasperation.

"Hey, it was your idea to wait *a month* between our last time and our wedding night. I thought you were crazy," he punctuated with a roll of his hips.

Erica growled.

"Past tense?" she bit his shoulder.

Robert groaned and pulled her gown up and over her head.

"Oh, you're crazy now and will forever be crazy, and I love you, my wife," he placed a mouth over one of her nipples while he pinched the other.

"Then take me *now*!" Erica demanded and popped him on the back of his head playfully.

Robert broke free of Erica's breast and looked down at his wife. She'd always been the most beautiful woman in the world to him, but lying there beneath him in nothing but pearls and her wedding ring with her flaming locks that were as untamed as she was, she'd never been more beautiful. She was his wife, and he was, indeed, the luckiest man alive.

Erica took advantage of her husband's appreciation and flipped him over so that she sat on top of him.

"These have to go," she expertly whisked his boxers down his legs and reclaimed her spot.

Robert couldn't stop laughing knowing that she will always surprise him.

"Now, Mr. Cunningham, I'm going to make love to *my* husband," Erica grabbed his length and positioned herself to accept him.

"Your husband wants nothing more, Mrs. Cunningham," he gasped as she slowly slid down his shaft and began to move.

Robert's hands found her hips and guided her speed. She loved the control he exercised to always make sure that she came first, even when she took the lead. The power from his hands heated her from the inside and fire threatened to burst from her skin.

Robert couldn't take his eyes off Erica as she rode him in perfect rhythm. Their bodies had always fit so perfectly together, and now, as his wife, they were even more perfect.

Erica leaned backward and pressed her full breasts toward the ceiling, knowing her husband could never resist an invitation. Tonight was no different. He released her hips and took both breasts in his large, strong hands and squeezed, holding on as she rode him faster and faster. She *loved* when he grabbed her like that, feeling the strength in his grip.

Seeing her gorgeous husband lost in his desire for her made her need to feel his lips. Erica leaned forward and swallowed his moans, drew more out with her tongue and swallowed them whole. Pressed against him like this, she knew that she couldn't hold on much longer. Erica felt the heat burst free from her core as she gave in to the flames. It was Robert's turn to swallow her cries. Then he wrapped his arms around her and held on for dear life as he followed his wife into the flames.

THE END

EPILOGUE

John Foster sat at the kitchen table as his wife, Amelia, nursed their newborn baby girl, Elizabeth. He was deep into the newspaper and his second cup of coffee when all of a sudden, he spewed it all over the kitchen table.

"What the hell?!?!" Amelia shouted while removing their daughter from the line of fire.

John shook his head.

"I'm sorry. I was…shit…look at this!" he said with surprise and showed Amelia the society page.

Amelia read aloud:

> *Randolph Spencer proudly announces the marriage of his daughter, Erica, to Robert Alexander Cunningham, III this past Saturday.*

She looked at the accompanying picture and understood her husband's reaction. Robert and Erica stood there smiling back at them from the photo in the newspaper, their love evident in their smiles.

"How the hell did *that* happen?" she asked more to herself that to John.

"I was wondering the same thing, and on top of it all, she's my boss' daughter?!?!" John shook his head.

Amelia started laughing uncontrollably, and John joined her.

"Who are we to deny them their happiness?" Amelia shrugged when she regained her breath. She looked down at their nursing daughter, who was now wide-awake and looked quite perturbed that her peaceful breakfast was being disturbed. "I mean, who knows, maybe our love rubbed off on them."

John still despised Robert for ever making a play for Amelia, but he couldn't deny his wife's happily-ever-after, love-conquers-all logic. And, though he was happily married, in love with and completely satisfied by Amelia, he couldn't help but flash back to the night of their threesome and how insatiable Erica had been. *Lucky man*, he thought to himself about Robert and then finished the thought with the hatred he still felt: *bastard*.

John went back to his coffee and newspaper, and Amelia hummed a lullaby to Elizabeth as she finished nursing.

There was love.

All was right with the world.

BONUS CHAPTER

Now for a sneak peek at Chapter 1 of the third book in The ALWAYS

Series, TRUE BLUE.

Enjoy!

Love,

Jae

TRUE BLUE – Book 3 of The ALWAYS Series

By

Jae Johnson

Chapter One

Amanda Samson was swimming near the top of a dream. Visions

of ink black hair and darkened brown eyes flashed through her

thoughts. The sting from an erotic spanking as she rolled against the

sheets made her sex clench. The smell of him –

"Oh, shit!" Amanda's eyes flew open. It wasn't a dream. Seeing

her ex-husband sleeping peacefully in the spot he'd spent eight years

in bed with her sent her into a full-scale panic.

"Get up. Get up. Get up!" She spat as she turned on the bedside

lamp.

Brock tried to shake the haze of sleep from his eyes as realization hit.

"What the –"

"It doesn't matter. What matters is that it's 5:30 in the morning, and Samantha will be up in half an hour. Get up, and get out. She can't…"

Brock cut her off with a finger to her lips. "I know. I know. It's okay."

Okay? She thought. What part of this is okay? Still, sitting there naked, smelling of sex and Brock, with his finger on her lips, it felt oddly…okay.

"Please, Brock," she began. "Samantha is in a really good place right now, and seeing us together so early in the morning will just confuse her."

"I'm going. Really."

And with that, he rolled to place both feet on the floor and in one smooth, economic move, her left their – her – bed.

Turning to face his ex-wife, Brock just grinned. She was still beautiful, even more so with her cheeks flushed and sex-and-sleep-tousled hair. The sheets she clung to her body silhouetted her, and he felt the familiar stirring in his cock. Before last night, he'd resisted the urge to touch her for the years since their separation, even though he'd wanted to. He'd wanted to comfort her, wipe away her tears and try to make her forget – try to make *himself* forget – what he'd done. But he hadn't, until last night.

"Amanda, last night was –"

"Don't, Brock. Just, please, get dressed. I'm going to take a quick shower. Please let yourself out, and don't let Samantha see you."

With that, she gathered the sheet around her for extra protection from his piercing eyes and headed toward the master bathroom. She caught sight of his smirk before shutting the door.

Amanda looked at herself in the bathroom mirror. Her brown eyes were bright; her cheeks were flushed, and her hair was a mess. Her lips were swollen and sore. Dropping the sheet, she got the full aftermath of last night. Her breasts were heavy, areolas and nipples flushed bright red. There were love bites on her hips. The worst was what she couldn't see, what she could feel. The sight of her ravaged body made her belly tense with heat that brought with it a flush of moisture to her sex.

Oh, this was *so* wrong. She hadn't let Brock touch her in three years. The divorce had been painful enough. After he'd lost his partner in the line of duty and then losing himself to grief, Amanda had tried to burn the pain away with handsome, steady, solid, Mitch, but after a year of trying with him, she still hadn't been successful.

Amanda rushed to the shower, needing to be cleansed with the hottest water she could stand. The hot water rushed over her body like a baptismal fount, and she grabbed her loofa, lathered it up and scrubbed, willing herself to forget. But the roughness of the loofa only reminded her of Brock's touch; the water only reminded her of his hot, wet kisses on her body. Succumbing, she let herself remember every detail of last night.

Last night had been…*different.*

She had just said goodbye to Mitch and settled onto the couch with a glass of wine. Samantha was tucked in bed after a fun night of games and pizza. They were solidifying into a comfortable family unit, something Amanda hadn't thought possible after the divorce from Brock.

A knock at the door brought her to her feet. Wondering what Mitch had forgotten, she opened the door. The sight of her ex-husband standing there looking tired and stressed made her choke down her swallow of red wine.

"Brock?"

"Is Samantha up? I know it's late, but I'd love to see her. Please." His strained voice was punctuated with a heavy brow. "I need to see her, Amanda."

"She's asleep, Brock. You know it's past her bedtime," but she couldn't deny the pleading in his voice or the pained look in his eyes at being denied a glimpse of his daughter. "Come in. You can look in on her if you want, but please don't wake her. She's had a long day."

Alarmed, Brock replied, "Why? Is she ok?"

"She's fine. She had a heavy day of tests at school. Then Mitch came over for pizza and game night. She was worn out and barely survived the bath before crashing in bed." Looking at the relief spreading his worry-worn face, she added, "She's fine, Brock. What's wrong?"

"Nothing. It's just been a stressful day – week – and I just needed to see my baby girl." With that, he headed down the hall to Samantha's bedroom.

He was lying. She had come to read his tells since the divorce, but she was too tired to fight.

Amanda followed Brock down the hall and stood beside him in

the doorway.

"God, she's growing so fast," he breathed in relief. "Remember when she was a baby burrito, nothing but a head and a blanket? Now look at her." Through all of the nastiness with their divorce, Brock always spoke of their daughter with the reverence of a proud father.

"That was ten years ago, Brock, but, yes, she's growing into a beautiful young lady."

"I wish I were around for more of it, that I hadn't –"

"Stop. We're not having this discussion anymore. Step in and kiss her goodnight if you want and then go, please. It's been a long day for me, too." Amanda left Brock in the doorway of their daughter's room and went back to her spot on the couch and gulped her wine. Tears always stung her eyes when he talked with such remorse, and she would be damned if he would see them.

"Thank you for letting me see her," he whispered as he came back down the hall.

"I'll never keep you from her. You know that. She adores you too much, and through all of your crap, you've always been a good father."

"Thank you." Brock meant it more than he could tell her. Not ready to leave, he offered, "The wine looks good."

"It is," was her only reply as she took a slow, deliberate sip. Emboldened by the wine, Amanda closed her eyes, tilted her head back and ran her tongue along her bottom lip.

"You're going to make me beg, aren't you?" Brock smirked. "Fine. May I please stay for a glass of wine? I could really use it after that week I've had."

Looking over the man who used to share her life, Amanda caved. His lips were curled up into a smile, but his eyes hid something dark. His stance was a little too rigid but visibly relaxed when she rose to walk to the kitchen. Soft footsteps let her know that he was following her, and she was instantly nervous with the thought of being in such a closed space with her ex. Yet, pouring his wine, she allowed herself a glimpse of him through her eyelashes.

He was still very handsome. He stood shorter than Mitch, but he was more muscular. Apparently, he still favored his evenings in the gym. He'd allowed his black hair to grow a little longer, though still a respectable length for a police detective. His eyes were a dark brown that would always have the power to peel back her defenses if she'd let them. His mouth -- now that was dangerous. It always had been.

Lush pink lips stretched over perfectly white teeth that could break into a smile that knocked many women – and men – off their feet. A light shadow of hair dusted his square jaw. Brock's usually impeccable attire was slightly off. His blue, silk tie was pulled open at the collar of his white dress shirt, top button undone to reveal a smattering of chest hair.

Running her tongue along her bottom lip again, Amanda made her gaze stop there. Wine and Brock were very dangerous, and she hadn't allowed herself to step into that territory for quite some time. Offering his wine without a word, she sauntered past him back to the living room and sank back down on the couch. Again, he followed and sat at the other end.

After a sip from his glass, "You know I've always loved this couch. When we were married, curling up to you with a glass of wine while Samantha played with her dolls was always my favorite part of the day."

"What?" Amanda stared at him with dangerously dark eyes. "How dare you." Anger now. "What gives you the right to sit here and reminisce about your 'favorite part of the day' and then go home and fuck whatever woman you've found after that ginger got married? I still can't believe you managed to talk me into going to her wedding with you!"

Rising, Amanda had every intention of throwing him and his glass of wine out.

"Stop." The command in his voice took her by surprise, and she stood still. He placed his wine on the end table and took hers to do the same. "Don't. Just please. Give me this one, nice, peaceful moment to just be. Please." In that moment, Brock took Amanda by the hand and pulled her to his lap. A gasp of surprise escaped Amanda's parted lips as she was closer to her ex-husband than she ever intended to be again. "You. Are. Beautiful."

With that, Brock crushed his lips to hers. Amanda's brain short-circuited. Angry tears threatened to spill from her eyes, and she pushed against his firm chest. She could feel the heat coming off of him in waves as his arms crushed her body against his. They still fit together. She felt it, knew it as her heart started racing. Her body betrayed her and molded into his. As his tongue darted out to caress her lips, she involuntarily opened for him receiving his kiss and giving it back feverishly.

Brock knew he shouldn't be kissing Amanda, shouldn't be

holding her so tightly, shouldn't be needing her like he needed his next breath. Still, he couldn't resist invading her mouth, tasting the sweet wine on her tongue. It had been so long since he felt at home; three years since he'd touched her body, and he still knew how to touch here. She had fought him, but she felt the same way he did in that moment.

Never leaving her mouth, Brock grabbed at her face and pulled Amanda closer. He slid one hand around to the nape of her neck to hold her in place while the other kneaded her breast through her t-shirt. Her answering moan rippled through them both. Nipples stood hard and ready and begged for his skillful touch.

Brock wrapped his strong arm around her waist and lifted her to straddle his lap. Even through her clothes, the feel of his cock on such an intimate part of her body made her tremble. He wasted no time ripping her shirt from her body and freeing her aching breasts. He whispered his appreciation against her skin before taking a hard peak into his mouth. One arm anchored her to him while the other stretched up her back. His hand found her long dark hair and pulled, causing Amanda to arch further into him. The twinge of pain from his teeth on her nipple traveled all the way to her belly, heating a spot only Brock could touch. Back and forth from nipple to nipple he worked patiently. His hot mouth closed around one and then the other, and she started grinding against the heat growing in her sex.

Brock immediately let go of her hair and took his mouth off of her. The absence of his touch made her whimper.

"Stop grinding or I'll take you over my knee."

Her eyes grew wide. Brock had always been a strong, confident lover, but he had never threatened her before. Still, as new as it was, part of her wanted to challenge him.

Amanda met his eyes with a slant of her own. "You wouldn't dare."

"Oh, honey." His answering smile was scary and delightful and hinted of such dark promise that she almost came right there. Brock scooped her up, still connected at the pelvis, in one swift move. He carried her down the hall to what was once their bedroom and tossed her on the bed.

"Remove your pants. Leave the panties," he ordered.

Another quiver. "And if I don't," Amanda leveled her chin at him and answered.

"If you don't, I'll wait even longer to let you come."

Dark promises flew through Amanda's mind as she stared up at Brock, once her husband and lover. There were flashes of him in this man who stood over her, but there were also new and exciting treats. She hesitated only a moment before wriggling her hips and freeing herself of her comfy yoga pants. Lying there in nothing but pink, lacy boyshorts, she was at his mercy.

"Undress me," his voice gravely and low.

There was no hesitation this time. Amanda stood and loosened his tie and let it fall to the floor. Her fingers moved to one button and then the next until they had skillfully opened his shirt. She ran her hands up his hard stomach, through his chest hair and then over his shoulders to remove the shirt. Locking his gaze, she ran a finger from one hip to the other just where his pants met his waist, and Brock groaned. She never took her eyes off his as she unfastened his belt, button and slid down the zipper to his pants. Dropping to her knees, she slid his pants down his legs, never breaking contact with his skin. She paused once at his impressive erection. Amanda ran her tongue over her bottom lip again, and he gasped. Sliding lower, she helped him step out of his pants, socks and shoes before standing.

Crawling onto the bed and sitting with the headboard to his

back, Brock pulled Amanda to the bed with him, leaving her on her knees. Brown eyes locked to brown, and the tension flared. He crushed his mouth to hers again. Her cleft was aching, and her clit was throbbing. Her panties were soaked with her arousal, and she needed to be touched. She needed Brock to touch her.

Brock broke their kiss again, and again she whimpered. He ran his hands up her back and pressed her to lie down across his lap.

Gazing in wonder over her ivory flesh draped over his lap, Brock was in heaven. The globes of her ass were full and soft and perfect. He slipped a hand between the pink lace of her panties and her skin, and she moaned. He felt it through his cock, and he needed her. After massaging her cheeks, he finally ventured to her waiting cleft, slipped a finger into the hot, wetness and growled.

"Your pussy is so wet for me. I can't wait to taste you. To feel you gripping my cock. Oh, Amanda."

He removed his finger, and Amanda felt empty.

"Please."

"Hush. I've got you," he purred.

One arm still held her back to his lap, his hot cock pressing up into her breasts. The other hand slid her panties down to her thighs.

Anticipation was killing her, and she wanted to question, plead and beg, but she kept quiet. She felt the strength in his hand as he massaged her cheeks again, and then there was a sting. He swatted first one cheek, then rubbed the spot and then hit the other. He dipped his hands into her sex and stroked, removed it and then hit her again. There was fire under her skin, in her pussy and behind her eyes. Each sting of pain spread into pleasure as she found herself rising to meet his hand. He alternated spanking with fingering her clit, her cleft and her opening. The pain gave way to pleasure and the pleasure to ecstasy.

"Your ass looks so hot all pink with my touch. And you're so wet. You're going to undo me, Amanda You've always been my undoing."

She heard his words, his appreciation, but all she wanted was his touch. One more, and she would come hard and fast, and she needed it.

"Please."

"Shhhh, honey."

Brock picked her up and laid her back. Once again whimpering at the absence of his touch, she was soon rewarded with his mouth on her clit.

"God, you taste better than I remember. So hot and sweet," he murmured against her flesh.

At that, she arched up into his mouth. He kissed her clit, the walls of her sweet pussy and plunged his tongue inside of her. He licked her from bottom to top and back again, over and over. Placing his mouth over her clit, he began to suck. As he sucked, he put first one finger and then two into her, and her breathing quickened. He stroked that wonderful bundle of nerves inside of her while his tongue and lips stroked her clit.

Amanda flew higher and higher. She has known his touch before, but this was more. There was more need, yet more control. With each flick of his tongue and each movement of his fingers, she climbed. She was going to fall, and it was going to be glorious.

"Come for me, honey."

With his permission, she jumped. She felt each surge of orgasmic pleasure rack her body. She bit her screams back so as not to wake her daughter, and she tasted blood on her lip. She rocked against his face and clenched around his fingers until each shudder was gone, and he licked slowly, softly, and savored every drop.

"You are so beautiful when you come. I've missed making you come for me," he whispered as he crawled up her body, kissing between words. "Look at me, Amanda. I want to see you when I put my cock in you. Don't close your eyes."

She nodded, and he took his cock in his hand and guided it to her opening. Sliding in one thick inch at a time was excruciatingly blissful. She felt herself open for him, stretch for him and welcome him back into her.

As Brock hit the end of Amanda, he knew he was home. Her cunt gripped him like a glove, and he felt it all through his body. He didn't know what to do about his current case or Mitch or anything, but he would do anything in the world to make sure that he could do this every night. They fit perfectly. And then he started to move.

As Brock moved in and out of Amanda, tears flooded her eyes. This was so wrong, but it was so right at the same time. Her body fell into sync with his. She knew what he wanted. He knew what she wanted. She met him thrust for thrust. Their bodies, covered in sweat, slid against each other, and her nipples reveled in the feel of his coarse chest. His mouth covered hers in greedy kisses, stifling both of their moans. She was climbing again, and this fall would be harder than the last. He stroked her, entered her, pounded her, and she fell. And fell. And fell. She gripped his body and screamed into his mouth. And he kept moving.

"I can't get enough of you, honey. I want more." He plunged again into her pussy, wet from two orgasms and growled. He sat up and angled her hips up to him and hit her deeper and used the pad of his thumb to rub her clit. Amanda fell again, completely shredded by his lust. When the last of her orgasm rocked her, he grabbed her by her hips and thrust once, twice and threw his head back in a silent scream. His face contorted, and she knew that it was all for her. He spilled his desire into her and fell to cover her.

Then they fell to sleep.

The heat from the shower had only awakened the heat from the night before, and all Amanda knew was that she had to get dressed and get Samantha ready for school. She climbed from the shower, towel dried her hair and threw on her bathrobe. Her only relief was in knowing that she didn't have to face Brock; he would be long gone by now.

Amanda glanced at the clock above the mantle. 6:15 a.m. Samantha would be up and in the kitchen already waiting on breakfast.

The smell of bacon froze Amanda in her tracks. Samantha knew better than to start without her.

"Samantha, baby, what –"

"Look, Mommy. Daddy came over early to make me breakfast!"

Brock looked at her and smiled. "Good morning, Sleepyhead."

ABOUT THE AUTHOR

Jae Johnson has graduated from spinning erotic tales in her head to putting them down on paper. A born-and-bred South Carolinian, she enjoys many different tastes and indulgences and, in the true fashion of Southern Hospitality, wants to share them all. Jae lives in Aiken, South Carolina with her very patient high-school-sweetheart husband, their beautiful daughter and their myriad animals.

Jae is a professional copywriter by day and a fantasy spinner by night. When not writing and being a wife and mom, Jae spends her time onstage with local community theatres losing herself in the fantastic art of make-believe. A few of her favorite onstage credits include *Chicago: The Musical* (Matron Mama Morton), *9 to 5: The Musical* (Judy), *Rabbit Hole* (Becca), *The Drowsy Chapperone* (The Woman) and *The Great American Trailer Park Musical* (Jeannie.)

Jae is a member of Romance Writers of America, the trade association for romance writers. She is also a member of RWA's special interest chapter for erotic romance writers, Passionate Ink.

Jae is available for speaking engagements, public appearances and interviews and is always thrilled to speak with reading and writing groups by telephone or Skype.

CONNECT WITH JAE

<u>Web:</u> www.jaejohnson.com
<u>Email:</u> fantasyspinner@gmail.com
<u>Facebook:</u> www.facebook.com/FantasySpinner
<u>Twitter:</u> JaeJohnson29801
<u>Instagram:</u> jaejohnson_author
<u>LinkedIn:</u> www.linkedin.com/pub/jae-johnson/92/120/b06/

www.ingramcontent.com/pod-product-compliance
Lightning Source LLC
Chambersburg PA
CBHW061324170626
46817CB00001B/302